One Night with the Werewolf

LYONNE RILEY

STORY INTRODUCTION

It's Emelia's twenty-sixth birthday, and she's invited everyone to celebrate her new promotion at work. But when her boyfriend Jason doesn't even show up, she discovers he's cheating on her. Devastated, Emelia's friends decide to give her a night out on the town—along with Jason's dad, Roscoe.

Roscoe might be in his late forties, but he can have a few beers and dance with the best of them. Now, he has to make up for what a jackass Jason has been. After drying Emelia's tears, the two find themselves drawn to each other.

When they both agree to it being "just one night," neither anticipates how deep that one night will go. But Roscoe has a secret—he's a werewolf, and it led to his last divorce. How can he possibly be what Emelia needs?

CONTENT WARNINGS

May contain spoilers.

- Graphic depictions of sex
- Age gap
- Surprise baby
- Discussion of abortion
- Knotting
- Transformed sex (as a werewolf)
- Consensual chase
- Pregnancy
- Birth

CHAPTER
ONE

think that maybe the day things were over with Jason was the day I thought he had the same good looks as his dad but none of the charm.

But I hold out. I'm a holder-outer. I will loyally wade with you into the storm if I think we have a good reason. After four years of dating Jason, it would take a lot for me to want to leave him. I see him as my future husband, my partner. He might not be the best boyfriend in the world, with how he forgets important things in my life, and he doesn't communicate well. And maybe we don't live together thanks to Jason's stonewalling, but I love him, just like I always have. Like I always will, because that's the kind of person I am. Loyal to the end.

I guess I just didn't expect the end to come so soon.

I'm lucky that my birthday falls on a Saturday this year, so no one will be rushing over from work or thinking about where they have to be the next morning. No, on this twenty-sixth birthday, I've just gotten a fantastic promotion at work and I am ready to party down.

As always, we meet at Elroy's, our favorite bar. Jason and I come here all the time, and it's one of the few places we hang out besides his house. I always go to his place because he doesn't like my roommate, Arin. I've never understood it—Arin is clean, polite, and a naturally generous person—but I've respected it. Maybe it's something about the fact Arin can shift into a unicorn at will.

So instead, I make the trip to his apartment most nights, which is a bit of a bummer as his roommates are all human men and don't take particularly good care of it. I'm lucky if I find only one sock on the bathroom floor.

Naturally, Arin is here at Elroy's with me, as are my other friends from college, Becks and

Harry. Then two friends from work show up, too: Kim, a human with pink hair, and Kimmy, a gorgon with the most lovely array of snakes on her head. Kimmy doesn't actually like the name "Kimmy" outside of work, but otherwise we would have no way to distinguish her from Kim —who was there first—and she hates "Kimberly" even more. So Kimmy it is.

It's so exciting to see everyone again that I jump from person to person, giving out hugs and trying to catch up quickly on recent life events. Of course, I just saw Kim and Kimmy yesterday, but it's always wonderful to see them outside of work and let our hair down a bit.

Then boots click on the hardwood floors. I glance up to find a tall man striding into the bar, the bright evening sun making it difficult to discern his features. But I know his walk, the shape of his shoulders, the sound of the heavy work boots he always wears—it's Jason's dad.

He glances around when he steps in the room, frowning. This is mostly a college bar, and the majority of the patrons are in their early- to mid-twenties. He's met us here a few times before for other events, like graduation or Jason's birthday, but I know he must feel like a fish out of water. Usually I see him at Jason's apartment when he stops by, or at dinner when he invites us over to his house.

I pull away from my friend Harry to run over and greet him.

"Roscoe!" His head jerks as he turns toward the sound of my voice. I halt just before hugging him because we aren't really on a hugging basis. I stick out my hand, and he gazes down at it with one eyebrow raised. Then, he extends his own hand, and we shake woodenly.

"Hey," he says smoothly. "Happy birthday." His stubble is thicker than usual today, a shading of salt and pepper across his jaw and chin to match his hair. He styles it with just a bit of gel, so it doesn't look greasy but ensures his straight part remains that way.

"Thanks. I'm glad you could make it." I went out of my way to invite Roscoe personally, knowing Jason would forget to tell him.

"Wouldn't miss it, Emelia," he says, his gaze trained on me. His green eyes are always striking with his dark hair. Jason got brown eyes from his mom, who I've only met once before. She lives in Indiana or Illinois or something like that.

I feel a blush rising in my face the longer we talk, so I quickly turn around and usher him to follow. "We're sitting over here."

Obediently, Roscoe follows along behind me, his hands stuffed in his jean pockets as we head around the bar for the two tables we've pulled together. We might have to add a third when Jason shows up, especially if he brings anyone with him. Sometimes his roommates will join us impromptu on an outing I thought was just for us.

I've gotten used to them being more or less appendages.

My friends all get up and greet Roscoe when he joins us. Awkwardly, he shakes hands with everyone before sitting down.

"You're Jason's dad, right?" Kim says, who's probably the oldest of us besides Roscoe.

"Yup."

"You look just like him." Kim surveys him like a predator sizing up a fat steak.

"Works that way sometimes," Roscoe says patiently. "He did get half of my DNA."

Kimmy snickers.

Conversation pivots to Jason, who should have been here twenty minutes ago. He's almost always late to things, though, so I'm not stressed about it yet.

We get all the introductions over with, and to my surprise, quiet Arin is the one who starts off the conversation by talking about the painfully hot bartender, a harpy with an incredible amount of jewelry. We all laugh and agree that she's an absolute smokeshow, and Kimmy starts encouraging Arin to go hit on her. Unfortunately, they are far and beyond too shy to do such a thing, so Harry takes it upon himself to suggest one of us approach the bartender on Arin's behalf, instead.

I love the sound of my friends all laughing together as Arin, flabbergasted, waves us off. "Oh, I would die of embarrassment," they say, covering their face. "No way."

We discuss plans for a new school to help young adults overcome social anxiety, which would clearly be a hit, but my attention wanders the longer we talk. Jason's now almost an hour late, which is late, even for him.

But I try not to keep my eye on the clock. He must have run into something along the way. He doesn't work on Saturdays, but there's always construction in this town, especially in the summer. He might have been out hiking with his roommates earlier today.

I realize then that I don't even know what his plans were. I was busy getting myself ready for the party. It occurs to me that maybe it's odd my boyfriend and I didn't do anything together on my own birthday. I just don't want to come across as clingy.

More time passes, and my friends buy me more drinks that I sip on while I wait. Luckily, Elroy's offers great pub snacks, so we order plenty of fried food to go around and soak up the alcohol. Martin, the bar manager, approaches me to say "Happy Birthday" and offers to play some of my favorite songs on the jukebox.

Roscoe is mostly quiet, his chair tilted back as he watches and listens without contributing. I hope he's not bored with our chatter.

An hour and a half has gone by, and still no sign of Jason. Everyone but me is drinking and having fun, and while I've got my happy face plastered on, I'm worried. Did he get into a car accident? Did he just... forget?

Finally, I get out my phone and text him.

> Hey, where are you? We've been here for a while.

But there's no answer. I wait another twenty minutes, thinking maybe he was just driving, but still—nothing.

When I look up, I find Roscoe watching me.

"Hasn't called or anything yet, has he?" It's not really phrased as a question, because we all already know the answer: my phone hasn't rung since he showed up two hours ago.

"No, but I'm sure he has a good reason," I answer defensively.

Roscoe gives me a flat look. "Why don't you call him up? Put him on speakerphone. I'll make sure he gets over here."

He says it like a command, and immediately I obey, tapping Jason's number and setting the phone on the table as it rings. I hope I don't regret this.

On the fourth ring, there's a long pause and a huff of breath. Then Jason's voice says—loudly— "Oh, hey."

I cringe at his impatient, annoyed tone of voice, as if I've interrupted something important by calling.

"We're all at Elroy's," I say quickly into the phone speaker.

"Hey Jason!" Kimmy calls out.

"Oh, what for?" Jason asks. His voice is slurred, like he's been drinking. I hear a woman giggling in the background.

"We're here for... my birthday?" Does he not remember at all that we had plans tonight? Does he even *know* it's my birthday? I told him about my promotion yesterday, and how this was a celebration of me moving up in the world, too.

"Where are you, Jase?" Roscoe cuts in. "You should have been here hours ago."

"Oh, hey Dad."

The woman on the other end of the line says, "Come on, get off the phone."

"Sorry," Jason continues. "I didn't realize your birthday party was tonight, Em."

"Well, it is." I try not to sound too put-out. He hates it when I *talk down* to him, which is pretty much any time I criticize him at all, so I try not to do it.

"Babe, can I take a raincheck? You're with your friends, right?"

"Yeah, she is," says an irritated Becks. She's been quiet this whole time, but now she sits forward to speak into the phone. "We can all hear you."

"Then you don't need me, right?"

Roscoe glares down at the phone, his eyes like razorblades. "Son," he snaps, "is there another woman with you?"

There's silence on the other end. Then we hear a second woman in the distant background calling out, "Where did that wine go?"

"Maybe," Jason answers with an awkward laugh.

Everyone at the table falls quiet. It's obvious what's going on, and I'm just the only one who's not willing to admit it.

"Are you having sex with that woman?" I ask, dreading what the answer will be.

"Yeah."

He just says it like it's no big deal. Tears rush to my eyes as silence follows. My face is getting hotter and hotter, until I think a volcano might be about to go off inside me.

"I didn't think I raised such a cruel man," Roscoe says at last, his eyes traveling to me. "Cheating on his woman in broad daylight."

I shake my head. I don't want him to tear down Jason right now. I just want this to be over.

"Enjoy your... whatever you're doing," I finally say. "Don't bother coming. Not that you were." Then I tack on, "We're over, Jason."

Jason sighs, then the line goes dead.

He didn't even have a parting word for me.

Nobody speaks as I pick up the phone and slide it back into my purse. The rock music playing in the background of Elroy's continues as if nothing happened.

"This is bullshit," Roscoe snarls, getting to

his feet. "I need to talk some sense into that idiot boy."

I grab his sleeve purely on instinct. He halts and glances down at me with his brows raised.

"Sorry," I say, letting him go. "Just that it won't do any good. You know what he's like. You catch him with his hand in the cookie jar, and he's going to pretend like the jar was never even there in the first place."

Roscoe hisses between his teeth. Probably because he knows I'm right. Confronting Jason will do no good, and neither of us has any clue where he is anyway.

"I know what you need," Kim says, standing up and waving an arm. "Barkeep! Another round for the birthday girl. She just dumped her boyfriend."

I feel like I'm the one who got dumped, but I don't correct her.

"Oh, damn, really?" The hot bartender from earlier hastily makes a pink concoction, even though I'm more of a beer girl, and brings it over to the table. "On the house. Sorry about the boyfriend."

I give her a grateful smile and take the cocktail with fresh rosemary on top, which does smell really good.

Talking resumes at the table as I drink.

"What an asshole," Kimmy says, crossing her arms. "I can't believe the sheer disrespect."

"I've never really liked him," admits Becks. "Sorry, Em."

I force a smile and nod, but inside, my world is collapsing.

Jason was my person. My everything. Or so I thought.

My friends go on to talk about all the things they never liked about Jason—which might have been nice to hear sooner in my relationship. Meanwhile, Roscoe hasn't spoken in his seat beside me. But as I stare down at the table with tears in my eyes, a hand brushes over my shoulder in a soothing circle.

"I'm sorry," he says in a low, scratchy voice. I know he was a smoker for a while, and you can hear it in his raspy tone. "My son is a fucking moron."

"It's okay."

"No, it's not." He sighs and releases me. "I want to say *forget about him*, but it's not that easy. You two were together a long time."

"Four years."

We were fresh out of college when we met at a party. I feel like my first drunken hookup with him, when he came within two minutes, should have been a red flag.

I am very good at ignoring red flags.

"And he just pissed all over everything," Roscoe says, shaking his head. "I want to say it started when his mom left, but I think he's always been this way. Selfish and inconsiderate."

Part of me is affronted that he would think of his son so poorly, but after tonight, I don't think he's wrong, either.

"Hey, you doing okay?" Arin leans over to check in. "Do you want to go home?"

"Don't go home!" calls out Harry. "Fuck that guy! Spend the night out with your friends, huh? Let us treat you nice since he won't."

"Yeah!" Kimmy says, joining in. "We can show you a good time, Em."

I glance around at all my friends, smiles on their faces, eager to have fun tonight. Then I look at Roscoe.

"You don't have to come," I say. "We're probably going to the club or something."

"Oh yeah? You don't think an old man can dance?"

Shit. I didn't mean to offend him.

"No, no, I'm sure you can. I just thought it might be boring, or..."

"How would going out to the club with a posse of hot young people be boring?" He grins. "Unless this is you trying to not invite me. Then I need you to be a bit more blunt."

I shake my head rapidly. "No, no! You're more than welcome. Right, guys?" I turn to my friends, and Kimmy is the first to pipe up, saying, "Yeah! Come on, Mr. Dad!"

"Name's Roscoe," he grumps, and everyone laughs.

CHAPTER
TWO

ROSCOE

That fucking asshole kid of mine.

I wasn't kidding when I said he's always been like this. I know, it's terrible of me, being his dad and all—but it's not surprising in the least that he would treat his sweet, soft-eyed girlfriend like this. I've always thought she's much too nice, too good for him, though I'd never say it out loud. I was surprised the first time I met her and Jason said, *This is my girlfriend, Em.*

Someone this kind and gentle had taken on Jason? At the time, I thought it'd be good for him, that it might push him out of his self-indulgent, arrogant persona and into his adult self. At the time, I never thought what a toll that would take on her.

He doesn't know how good he had it.

I put on my best impression of a smiling face as everyone finishes their drinks at the bar and pays up. I like how Emelia's friends rallied by her side to give her a fun night out on the town. Maybe I'm a bit of a douchebag for inviting myself along when this really should be a young person's game, but at the same time, I feel like I should make up to her for how horrible Jason was tonight. As the representative of the Daniels family.

Maybe I can help Emelia forget about my dickhead kid for one night, and then I'll never see her again. It feels like a fitting farewell for all the lovely Christmases and Fourth of Julys we've had as a family. I've always enjoyed her company —she's honest and genuine, but never mean or harsh. It's not a common trait in people nowadays, to be so authentic and kind without trying. But Emelia has one face, her real face, and she always wears it.

I can admire that in a person.

The night air is perfectly warm, the ideal summer evening, with just a faint breeze. I wore my nice leather jacket tonight, which I'm sure I'll regret when we get to the club and there are bodies pressed in all around me. But I don't trust a coat check. My jacket's been with me ever since I became what I am.

The kids chitchat while we walk. Though I don't add to the conversation, I do stay close by Emelia. It isn't cold, but her arms are wrapped tight around herself, and I can't tell if she's cold or sad.

Probably both. I should offer her my coat, but it's only a few blocks to the club, since we can hear it two streets over. There's a short line out front, and we get in it with Emelia at the front.

"You been cryin', babe?" asks the bouncer, a big ogre with a single horn on his forehead, frowning down at her from his stool as he looks over her ID.

"A little," she admits.

"I hope your night gets better." He glances at me as I approach. "Oh, I don't need your ID. But you're not the one who made this girl cry, right?"

I shake my head. "It was my son."

The bouncer stares at me, then snorts and waves for us to go inside.

We beeline for the bar, and now it's my turn to buy her a drink.

"Ready?" I ask, as her friends get IDed out by the door.

"For what?"

I wave a hand, and a bartender immediately comes over. "For a great night. Can you grab this woman an amber ale, please? One for me, too."

He nods and takes off.

"How did you know?" Emelia asks. "About the amber ale?"

"You always order it at dinner. And you keep some at Jason's house."

Yeah, so maybe I pay too close of attention to Emelia's habits. I also know that she loves fried chicken more than anything—not like microwave chicken tenders, but real, honest-to-god triple-dipped fried chicken—and she's really not a cocktail person unless someone puts it in front of her. Then she smiles and nods like she did tonight.

It's too bad I won't see her again after this. I discovered a really great chicken and waffles place on the other end of town that I'm sure she doesn't know about. Maybe I'll tell her before we wrap up.

"Huh." She gives an approving nod as the beer arrives. "Thanks, Roscoe."

"No problem."

We take our plastic cups as the rest of the cavalry arrives. Once everyone's got a drink, we head toward the open area near the DJ where people are dancing and lights are flashing. It's not really my thing to get up on the dance floor and shake it, so I head off to one side to grab a table and sit down, planning to people watch for a few hours.

I'm surprised when Emelia joins me, as do her two friends, Harry and Arin. I made a point of introducing myself to each of them and re-peating their names a few times until I had them memorized.

"You should be dancing," I tell Emelia. "Get-ting messy. That's what you call it now, right?"

"I hate dancing with a drink. I'd rather drink the drink, *then* go get messy on the dance floor."

Hm. I have to admit it makes sense.

We watch the other three, who introduced themselves as Becks, Kim, and Kimmy, head out into the throng, waving at us as they go by. Look at me, remembering all those names. Emelia waves back, sipping her beer.

"Thanks for the drink," she says, as if we've

run out of things to say to each other that aren't about Jason.

"No problem. I've been working a lot of overtime, so it's not a big deal."

"Are you still with that surveying company?" she asks. Ah, so she remembers. I think I've only mentioned what I do once or twice, because Jason is usually dominating the conversation. That boy loves to talk about himself.

"Sure am. We've been busy lately. Lots of new construction."

She nods. "The city's growing fast. It's kind of sad to see—all these fun old spots going away and becoming apartment buildings."

Interesting. So she's not in favor of development. I agree with her, but at the same time, it's my job and has been my whole adult life.

"You missed about a dozen others before you got here," I tell her. "The city is always changing. You can't stop it. But new places to enjoy will pop up somewhere else."

"Yeah, but the history. Like Elroy's. There's something special about that bar. I think this town would lose something if it disappeared and became a high-rise."

I see where she's coming from, and I appreciate that she's concerned with such things.

"But there's a big demand for housing, too," I say. "Rent is skyrocketing and everyone needs a place to live. We can expand up, or we can expand out. If we expand out, we take more land away from wild areas. I would rather go up."

Her mouth opens like she's going to speak, but then she closes it again, tilting her head at me.

"Good point," she finally says.

I nod. "Cities are actually very smart in that way. If we were really the advanced species we think we are, everyone would live in a massive apartment building that recycles water through a series of fish tanks and plant nurseries."

Wow, I sound like a goddamned geek. But both Emelia and Arin are listening raptly while Harry plays around on his phone.

Men these days.

"That makes sense," Arin says after a moment. "I agree with you now, I think."

"But I just hope they don't take Elroy's," Emelia adds. "Any place but Elroy's you can turn into a skyscraper, okay, Roscoe?"

I laugh. "Not my decision, but I'll keep it in mind."

After a few more minutes of chatter, Emelia finishes her beer. I've already polished off mine, as experienced as I am in drinking a lot of beer way too fast, and so I get up to fetch us more.

"Yeah!" Emelia says, hopping to her feet. "I didn't think you'd want to go out and dance."

Looking at her radiant smile, her eyes still red from crying, I don't have the heart to tell her I was just heading over to the bar to refill.

"Sure," I say. "I'm an old man, but I can dance."

Her smile fades. "You're not old. I don't know why you'd call yourself that."

She seems almost... affronted.

"I'm approximately twenty-one years older than you are," I say. "That's when Julie and I had Jason."

Emilia gets a look on her face like she just ate a lemon. "I don't want to think about Jason right now." She grabs the sleeve of my leather jacket and pulls on it. "Let's go out there and see how those joints of yours move."

The dance floor is packed densely enough now that we have trouble finding her friends, so eventually, we give up. Instead, Emelia and I dance awkwardly side by side, simply grooving with the music while others dance far more wildly around us. A couple nearby are face to face, making out while they rub their hips together.

I was never much of a dancer in my heyday, either. But I did like that part of it—holding someone while you both rock in time with the music. It reminds me of my wedding to Julie, when we were still happy together.

Before the bite.

"Roscoe?" Emelia calls over the pounding music. "Are you okay?"

"Just thinking."

"I am, too." Her eyes are misty again, and that's not good. She should be distracted, but her friends aren't here—so that leaves it up to me.

I take her hand in mine, glancing down at her for permission. She nods, so I loop my other arm around her back.

"This is the only dancing I know how to do," I tell her as I bring her in a bit closer, but not too close. "It's probably not what you're looking for."

She shakes her head, both eyebrows up to her hair. "No, no, this is fine."

We dance along to the music that way, probably looking like a couple in our sixties trying to groove with the cool kids. But eventually, I feel

Emelia's hand relax in mine, and her own arm snakes around my waist.

"Hey, thanks," she says.

"For what?"

"For keeping me company. We lost Arin, never found the Kims, and who knows where Becks went." She sighs. "I still can't believe it."

I nod, just listening to her over the frantic beating of the speakers.

"It's like it meant nothing to him. Nothing at all. He couldn't have cared less." She sniffles, leaning her head against my chest. "I knew it, I think. That he had other people. Deep in my gut. But I wasn't willing to admit it."

I'm sick to my stomach, thinking that my own kid would behave so callously toward someone as gentle as Emelia.

"I feel like somehow, it's my fault," I say with a sigh. "I raised that kid. There must be a reason, something I did."

"Sometimes nature is stronger than nurture." Emelia puts a hand on my chest to comfort me. "I'm sure you did your best."

I just want to hold her tighter as she starts sniffling again, but I don't want to cross any lines while we dance here politely. But then Emelia turns her face to cry into my jacket, and I pull the sides away so she can reach my shirt, which is much softer.

She sniffles, then takes the invitation and wraps both arms around me as she cries against my chest. I close the jacket around her, rocking her back and forth to the beat of the music.

Eventually, her sobbing slows down, and she backs away from me, rubbing her eyes.

"I'm sorry," Emelia says, a sad smile lifting her lips on one side. "I got your shirt soaking wet."

"It's fine." I close the jacket again now that she's put some distance between us. "Do you feel better?"

She laughs. "No. Not really. I need to drink more."

I smirk and pull out my wallet. "I can help with that."

CHAPTER
THREE

Beers in hand, we eventually reunite with the Kims, though at least one of my friends is still missing in action. Arin and Harry are locked in conversation, and I didn't think Harry was their type, but you learn new things about people every day.

Don't think about Jason. Don't think about Jason.

Roscoe must sense that my mind is wandering because he taps my elbow, leading me back to our table. We drink more beer as my friends ask him all kinds of questions, like he's a novelty. And I suppose he is, unshaven and wearing his heavy boots, two decades older than any of us. His leather jacket wonderfully complements his broad shoulders and contrasts the bit of salty seasoning in his hair.

I never thought older men were attractive until now, but I can't take my eyes off him. Maybe it's beer goggles. Maybe it's the fact he's been so kind to me tonight, when I never got much of a read from him before. He's opened up to me to make me feel better, and I genuinely appreciate that kind of human connection.

Plus, he let me cry into his shirt. You don't get that every day from a stoic man with a lot of stubble.

After a while, the conversation moves on and people start saying goodnight. First it's Kim, then Becks—who reappeared after an hour—and then Kimmy. Harry has been hitting on Arin, but Arin is as shy as they get and hasn't picked up his messages yet.

"Another drink?" Roscoe asks, getting up from the table. "Then more dancing is on the docket, I think."

I grin, because that's exactly what I want to do, even though I know the whole dancing thing makes him uncomfortable.

"Thank you. I really should buy the next round."

He looks like I've shat on his carpet. "No honorable guy lets a girl buy her own beer on her birthday. And you got a promotion, didn't you? That was part of the invitation."

I cover my cheeks with both hands. "Yeah. They made me a regional manager. It's like a whole two steps up from where I was before."

Roscoe's smile is broad and genuine. "Congratulations, Emelia. I'll be back in five seconds." Then he takes off, literally jogging, toward the bar to get us more beers.

Harry and Arin are exchanging phone numbers. "Are you coming with me?" asks Arin. "I'm thinking of leaving."

I frown. "So soon? But we're still having fun." The world might be swimming a bit, but I'm finally having a great time not thinking about Jason.

"You and Roscoe are having fun, you mean." Arin waggles their brows.

I swat them with my purse. "It's not like that."

"All right, if you say so."

I glance at Harry, who clearly has tried hard, but Arin is too sweetly dense.

"I'll walk you to your Uber," he says, almost morose, as Arin calls one.

Roscoe's surprised when he gets back to find the table is now empty of everyone but me.

"Your friends left?" he asks.

"Yeah. Tired. It's late."

"Pssh." Roscoe rolls his eyes. "It's barely one in the morning. The night is young. I thought the youths stayed out later than this."

I like that he's, well, not vanilla at all. He clearly was a party guy in his day. Maybe still is. It's not like your life ends at forty.

As we drink our beers, I can't help feeling like this night has become almost a date. But I'm here trying to forget about Jason, not get busy with his dad.

Still, as the night goes on and we abandon our empty plastic cups to head out into the throng of dancers again, I start to notice things —how he moves with such strength hidden beneath his skin. How he puts an arm out to protect me as we work our way through the crowd. How he smells? A tantalizing mixture of plain soap and plain deodorant and his own delicious scent.

As we start dancing again, his arm around me and our other hands linked, I could simply lick the sweat off his neck.

Yes, he's hot. He's definitely hot, and he's

also definitely pulling me closer as we dance until my cheek is resting against his chest and his chin is perched on top of my head. He holds me like that to the beat of a wild song, as if the bright-colored world around us doesn't matter at all.

I could simply sink into him like a soft mattress. His heart is beating much faster than his smooth movements give away, and I wonder if I'm doing to him anything like what he's doing to me. I want to bury my face in his armpit, he smells so good. I want to see what he looks like underneath that leather jacket and plain white Fruit of the Loom shirt.

This is my ex-boyfriend's dad we're talking about, and we're pressing ourselves even closer together, our hips gently brushing up against each other. I almost don't give a shit, and that should frighten me, but the beer has gone right to my brain and I'm happy and loose and nobody else is even *here*. It's just me and Roscoe, alone, surrounded by strangers.

I peek up at him, wanting to see what's on his face, if it might give away how he's feeling about this. When I do... I see yellow.

Yellow eyes peering back at me. The green is

now wholly gone, and the bright yellow glows in the dim light on the dance floor.

"Whoa," I say, not sure what I'm looking at. Immediately, the yellow fades, and his eyes return to green again.

Did I just imagine that? Does he have some kind of contacts in?

Roscoe licks his lips, his gaze darting away from mine nervously, then back again. "Do you want this?"

"Want what? To dance with you?" I pull him closer. "Yes." And then, because I'm horny and feeling bold, I rub my crotch against his.

Roscoe's eyes practically roll back in his head, and his hands grip my hips.

"Emelia," he rasps. "That's dangerous territory."

"Is it?" Now I'm feeling a bit coy and sassy, too. That's not usually me, but right now... "Does it make you want to do dangerous things to me?"

His answering expression of shock almost shuts me down, but I remain firm in my question. Slowly, Roscoe nods.

"Yes." He leans his head down, and his voice is most certainly a *growl* in my ear. "Yes, it does."

His hand coasts from my hip to my back,

then down over my ass. He inhales sharply, his hips jerking in a way that seems entirely involuntary. The friction is welcome, and I want his hand to keep traveling south, down between my legs. I'm warm there—*so* warm—and all I need is for him to touch me. He pauses where it is, though, and then he squeezes with his firm fingers. Reflexively, I grind against him, and Roscoe grunts.

"You're drunk," he says, though he squeezes again as if his mouth and his hands belong to two separate people. "We shouldn't."

"You're drunk, too. And who says?" I trail my hands up his chest. "Nobody's here who would judge us."

If he turns me down, I'll probably cry like a baby. I can't handle two rejections in one night.

"True." Roscoe curls his other arm around me, keeping our lower bodies rooted together as we sway to the music. It's quite noticeable when his erection nudges me, and I make sure to rub myself over it, hopefully tantalizing him under his pants.

When his hold on me tightens, I think I've succeeded.

Growing bolder, my palms skim back down his body to his jeans, which are held up by a thick leather belt. Below the belt, I brush over where his dick is hiding underneath, and I watch Roscoe's face as he grits his teeth.

"That's damn good," he murmurs, his body responding to mine. I keep my hand hidden between us, but I probably shouldn't be getting him off in public.

"Can we go?" I ask suddenly. "Please?"

Roscoe leans backward so he can look down at me. "You're sure that's what you want?"

"I understand if you don't." My voice wobbles as I say it, because yes, I would understand, but I wouldn't like it. "I'm probably just upset, and I don't want to use you—"

"Use me." His grip stiffens around me. "Use me, Emelia. Make yourself feel better. If that's the purpose I serve, I'm more than happy to be that for you."

My eyes feel tight, but not because I'm sad. It's the way that I feel understood by this gorgeous man with sprinkles of gray in his dark hair. How he actually *sees* me.

"Thank you," I whisper, and I know he can't hear it over the music, but I think he can read my lips because he nods and tips his head down to kiss my forehead.

Oh, do I love that.

I grab his hand in mine and pull him off the dance floor, eager to get the hell out of this place and go somewhere we can be alone.

"Where are we going?" Roscoe asks as he obediently comes along with me.

"Leaving. Maybe your place?" I glance over my shoulder at him for confirmation. He lifts his brows.

"Sure, we can go there. It's a ways away."

"I know where you live. I just got a big raise, so I'll pay for the Uber."

He lets out a resigned sigh, but he's smiling. "All right. Let's go."

I don't release his hand as we head out into the cool night air. Well, cool relatively speaking. It's late August, nearing the end of summer soon, so it's late enough in the year that I'm a little bit chilly.

"Here," Roscoe says, taking off his leather jacket. He steps behind me to drape it over my shoulders. "Now call us that taxi."

Doing as I'm told, I tap for a ride and I'm lucky that there's a car close by. Then I sneak my hand into Roscoe's. I know what we're about to do isn't necessarily intimate, necessarily affectionate, but I feel affection for him right now and I want to show it.

He doesn't miss a beat, gripping my hand in return as if to comfort me, to assure me it's okay to ask for it.

Finally, the Uber appears at the curb, and we both climb into the back. I resist the urge to sit in his lap, and then we buckle ourselves in responsibly as the car pulls away. Still, though, Roscoe is holding my hand, and when I glance up, I find him staring straight ahead with a slight smile tugging at his lip.

Boy howdy, do I like his face. He has some of Jason's features, but on him they are less soft and more rugged, with a bump in the bridge of his nose that makes me wonder if he's broken it before. And then, of course, there's that handsome stubble, the square jaw that isn't lined with baby fat, and the crinkles at the corners of his eyes that deepen when he grins.

I really could just eat him.

Feeling adventurous, I abandon holding hands and instead, my fingers drift down to his jeans, where I rub over the slight lump still there. Roscoe bites his lip and holds in a breath, watching me as I touch him just outside the driver's line of sight. I know I shouldn't, but I can't help teasing him.

I think watching this man come undone might be my life's greatest accomplishment. I can't wait.

CHAPTER
FOUR

ROSCOE

This woman is going to wreck me in the best way possible, I can already tell. She's sensual, soft, and giving while also being demanding, telling me exactly what her needs are. We just have to wait until we get back to my house, and then I'll figure out getting my car tomorrow.

I really should download that "Uber" app.

Emelia doesn't relent in stroking me through my jeans, which is making me harder and harder. At this rate, I might just come in my pants, which is not at all how I want to start this.

Luckily, the beer in my system is dimming

my senses, so I think I'm in the clear by the time we get off the highway and head into the neighborhood.

I live on the edge of the city along the railroad tracks, just before the suburbs take over. Here, the houses are old and many of them rundown, though I've tried to keep my own in good condition. It's not where Jason grew up—Julie and I sold that house when we divorced—but it's where he spent many of his middle and high school years while we shared custody. He still has a room there with all his old posters up on the wall, though he hasn't used it in eons. I really should just convert it to a guest room, or maybe an office space.

At last, the Uber arrives at my single-story house. It's not much to look at it, with a plain grass yard that I keep watered, most of the weeds removed from between the gaps in the sidewalk. I get out first, offering Emelia my hand to help her out, too. The driver says nothing as he pulls away, and I'm sure he was wiser to our backseat shenanigans than he let on.

Emelia is still gripping my hand as we stand there on the front walk, the porch looming over us.

"Show me in?" she asks in a quiet voice, and I

wonder if she's regretting her decision to come here. Perhaps she's just nervous.

I settle an arm around her waist and lead her to the steps. "Happily. Not much to look at, as you know."

"It's yours," she says, voice slurring. My own is too, and I'm not walking completely straight. This could all be a very bad idea, a voice in the back of my mind suggests, but I'm far too hungry for this woman now to stop the train from barreling forward.

Inside the front door, though, Emelia transforms. The second it clicks closed, she pushes me up against it, her hands finding their way under my jacket. She presses herself against me, tilting up her head so our faces are only a few inches apart.

Goddamn, she's beautiful. So fucking beautiful. Her hair is the most peculiar shade of brown with a smattering of red in it. She has a petite nose, full lips, and eyes as big as a doll's, with long lashes to match. Her cheeks are perfectly freckled, as is the bridge of her nose, like someone painted them across her face.

And she clearly wants me to kiss her. What kind of monster would I be if I didn't oblige? I know this can't go any further than tonight, so I'll make it the best night possible.

Emelia lets out a soft moan the moment my lips touch hers. It's like we're electrified, and this mere touch sends shockwaves into both of us. Now it's my turn to put the pressure on her, bending her back as my arms snake around her, holding her up as my soft kiss turns into a ravaging.

Her mouth is so pliant as I invade it, so yielding as I conquer it with my own lips that I can't hold in my groan. I wonder if all of her tastes as good as her mouth does. I wonder if the rest of her gives the same way.

My hand curls under the back of her head as I dominate her, fucking her throat with my tongue, then nipping her lips before gently soothing them. I've been smelling Emelia all night, drinking in the floral scent of her shampoo and contrasting fruity scent of her de-odorant, so I notice the moment that scent changes.

She's aroused—very aroused, and it's perme-ating the room. Even when I'm human, my senses retain some of my other form, and breathing in the smell of her weeping pussy is enough to turn on the animal inside me.

Without asking, I curl my hands under Emelia's butt and lift her into the air, hiking her up so her thighs are slung over my hips. She doesn't stop kissing me, even as she squeaks in surprise, so I think she's happy going along for the ride.

I carry her easily through the living room and then down the hall to my bedroom. We startle my black cat, Salem, and he darts out from under the bed and into the hall as we enter.

"Bye, kitty," mutters Emelia before she goes back to kissing me, her legs wrapping tight around my waist.

I don't bother closing the door behind us. It's not like anyone else lives here.

Keeping Emelia in my arms, I navigate to the bed and sit, which produces a situation where her ass is now resting on my lap, her legs spread around me. If there were no clothes between us, I could just lift my hips and—

Calm down, Rutting Roscoe. I know the animal is horny, but the woman needs to be ready for me.

We continue making out like teenagers as my jacket slides off her shoulders onto the floor. My hands explore her on their own, tracing her sides, her hips, her ass. It's still dark in the room, which is good, though there's a faint hint of streetlamp coming in the window. Just the right amount of light so she won't be able to get a good look at me when I take my pants off.

Emelia pulls back, and at first, I think I've done something wrong—but then she grabs the bottom of her shirt and peels it up over her head, tossing it away like it offended her. Now her tits are out, held up by a cute pink bra with white hearts on it, just a hint of her nipples showing over the top of the cups.

Damn. They are nice tits.

I don't think twice before I reach around her and pluck open the clip on the back, causing the bra to slip down her arms. Emelia grins as she flings that away, too, not caring at all where it lands.

"Now you," she says, lifting her hands to cup her breasts. She's putting them on display for me, and her blush-colored nipples are peaked and tight.

While she's occupied touching herself, I do as I'm told, yanking up my shirt and then dropping it to the floor. When I glance back at Emelia, she's rubbing her fingers over her nipples, gazing at my chest with her mouth slightly open.

I try to stay fit, going on runs and getting to the gym as often as I can with my work schedule. It's not like I have much else going in my life besides taking care of Salem and fixing cars. But by the look on Emelia's face, you'd think she just saw God.

"Wow," she finally says. "You're fucking hot."

I didn't think I was the type of person to blush, but that's definitely turning my neck and face warm. That's certainly the first time anyone's ever said that to me.

Her hands move from her own chest to mine, where she runs her hands down over my nipples to my abdomen. It clenches reflexively, and her eyes get even bigger. I think she likes what she sees. But I'm done waiting. The scent of her has become overwhelming, and soon, very soon, I need to taste her.

Holding her around the hips, I flip us over on the bed, and in a panic, Emelia clings to me around the neck like a monkey. I kiss her again as I lower her onto her back, then reach up the bed to grab a pillow for her. When I tuck it under her head, she makes a confused little frown.

"Get comfortable," I tell her, my voice coming out low and thick.

"For what?" she asks, but I ignore the question, sitting back so I can get a good look at her. Her skirt is cute, but I'm not sure how to go about taking it off.

"There's a zipper," Emelia says finally, amusement dancing on her face. She reaches for an invisible zipper on the side and pulls it down, revealing a perfect slice of pale hip. My mouth waters, and I grab the skirt and slide it the rest of the way off her legs. Now only her underwear remains in the way of what I want.

Thankfully, she doesn't ask me to take off my own jeans. She's merely staring at me, waiting for *me* to decide what comes next. I am not surprised to find that Emelia is meek and submissive even in bed, waiting to be told what to do.

"Underwear too," I tell her, and right away, she falls back on the bed to peel them down her thighs. Then I can really see her—the perfect globes of her breasts, the heaving of her chest as she pants with arousal, the neatly trimmed pubic hair that exposes her pink sex. She has a small clitoris, and the lips of her pussy are already pinkish and swollen, from what I can see in the dim light. I can surely make out much more with my night vision than she can. Right now, I hopefully look like nothing more than a shadow.

Now that Emilia's exposed to me, I crouch over her, kissing her again while my fingers slide down her sternum to her perfect tits. Her nipples are rock hard, and when I tease them, flicking them back and forth, she moans into my mouth. She's so supple and responsive, it'll be my absolute pleasure to fuck the daylights out of her.

No knot, I think, reminding myself.

I trace the path of my hands with my mouth, kissing away from her lips, down her chin to her throat, where I pause to lick and nip and suck. Emelia shudders and fists her hands in my hair, and I move on so I don't leave a mark. I don't want her to have to explain that.

Making my way to her left breast, I bring her nipple into my mouth and lick it, swirling my tongue around, imitating what I'm going to do in just a moment. Her back arches, and so I suck harder, like an infant seeking out food. I grab her other breast and massage it as I go, trying to hit all her erogenous zones at once.

Fuck. I can't take it anymore. I release her nipple with a *pop!* and continue down her belly, kissing the whole way. When I reach her pelvis, her thighs part for me of their own accord, and finally, my prize is revealed.

"I'm going to fuck you with my tongue," I tell her. "I'll make you sing, Emelia."

She lets out a gasp at my words. "Please. Yes. I want that."

I'm glad she's so eager for me, vocal in telling me so.

I lick my chops before positioning myself between her legs, lifting her thighs to get her good and wide for me. Her pussy gleams in the low light, a drip of wetness slipping out of her. The first thing I do is lick that up, and it's even better than I imagined. She tastes of salt and musk and *woman*, delicious, red-blooded woman, with a sweet flavor that makes her even more delectable. My tongue drags up, over her labia to the small clitoris I saw before.

Emelia's hands clutch the blankets the moment I touch it. She must be sensitive, so I make another lap around her pussy before returning to it, stroking it gently with the tip of my tongue. She squirms again, letting out a moan this time.

That's when I give in. I can't tease anymore, not when I need to eat her so badly. I suck her clit between my lips, and her thighs shake. I pull out every trick in the book, seeing how frazzled I can get her before I go to the next phase. Soon she's moaning, clutching my head in her hands so her nails are digging into my scalp, her thighs clenching tighter and tighter as I get her closer to her finish line.

Time to seal the deal. While she's distracted by her pleasure, I bring my hand up and lick my middle finger, then explore downward, through the petals of her pussy, until I find her entrance. She's so wet that it easily glides in.

"Oh, Roscoe!" she cries out, nearly her whole body lifting off the bed. I plunge the finger in deep, and Emelia responds, another feral sound of pleasure pouring from her lips. I could just drink them all up.

It only takes a few seconds of this before she's moaning and whimpering, her body trembling underneath me, her thighs tightening around my head. I move my finger faster, ready for her to burst, waiting to sip every last drop of her before I fit my cock inside her.

"Ah!" Emelia lets out a high-pitched squeal as suddenly, her pussy clamps down around my hand, and she gushes. She fucking *gushes* for me, spilling over my finger, which means that somehow, even in a drunken haze, I managed to make her squirt. I keep going because I know she has more in there, licking her faster, fucking her harder with my finger even as she whines and thrashes.

Then, as I suspected she would, she peaks again. She clenches even tighter, and this time, her cry is full-throated.

Perfect. Now, I think, she's ready for me. And I'm going to enjoy every last second of having her.

CHAPTER
FIVE

EMELIA

have never, ever come like that in my life. Even before I met Jason—he wasn't the most attentive lover, and only rarely ate me out—I've never had an orgasm like that one.

Or was it two orgasms? One and a half orgasms? I have no idea. But it was like a small wave that lifted me into an even bigger one, sending me free-falling. I almost forget where I am because I'm wasted and my brain is swimming with happy sex juice.

Then Roscoe rises above me, and I realize he's still wearing his pants. Damn, how did I forget that? I want to see him like he saw me.

When I reach for them, though, he grabs my hands. His teeth look sharper in the low light than I remember.

"Turn around," he says in that gruff voice, and instantly, I'm even wetter. Just the way he talks cranks my dial. His tone brooks no argument, so I obediently turn around on the bed, falling forward onto my hands and knees.

I would have loved to suck his cock a little after what he just did for me, but something in Roscoe's eyes told me we're past that now. He's almost... animalistic, if I were to pick a word. The way he climbs up onto the bed on his knees, panting heavily, hot breaths against my ass, I feel like a bitch in heat about to be mated.

I don't think twice about it as a soft, rounded object slips between the folds of my pussy. I'm slick, and his finger opened me up enough that immediately, the head of his cock slides through.

"Oh, fuck," I say, gripping the blankets as he asks me to open for him. He remains just barely sheathed in me, but the instant stretch is so glorious that I already need more.

"How's that, Emelia?" Roscoe asks, sounding almost hoarse with need. "Do you like the feel of my cock?"

"Yes!" I don't have to think before answering. "I love it. I need it."

"You need it?" He pushes in a fraction deeper, then retreats. "Does this sweet little pussy want all of me?"

I nod feverishly. "Yes, please, Roscoe. All of you."

Then I get my wish. He shoves himself in, sliding through me in one smooth motion, until he's seated. I cry out as my whole body stretches to accommodate him, swallowing him up as fully as I can. And god, does he feel incredible, smooth and soft and yet firm in all the right ways. When he draws back, the sensation of his cockhead dragging along the inside of me almost makes my arms give out.

Damn, in just one stroke, he feels better than any man or woman I've ever been with. If only I could have seen his dick first, because it *feels* absolutely beautiful. I bet it's the prettiest penis on the whole planet.

He almost leaves me completely before plunging back in, not too fast, not too hard, but the perfect amount of everything. He stops before fully bottoming out, almost like he's afraid of going all the way. That thought, though, flees my mind as he starts to really use it.

He glides in and out, establishing a smooth pace that has me scrunching up the blankets under my hands and moaning into the pillow that used to be underneath my head. His hand smooths down my ass, squeezing my ass cheeks and examining them like he's in no rush.

Is this what it's like being with an older man? There's no frenetic jerking, no hasty chase toward the orgasm. It seems like he's purely enjoying it, burying himself in me and then sliding back again. He slows down for a short time, letting me feel every inch of him as his hand snakes over my hip and around me, then down between my legs.

When he brushes my clit, he speeds up. Oh god. No one's ever done that to me during doggy style. Now he's thrusting fast, making sure to angle up his cock as if he knows exactly where to find my G-spot.

"Fuck, oh fuck," I find myself chanting as he brushes past that spot again and again, his fingers rubbing over my clit with the same steady rhythm as his hips are driving into me. "I'm going to come, Roscoe, I'm going to—"

"Say my name again."

"Roscoe!" I cry it out, because damn, it feels

good to shout it. He groans behind me, then emits a sound that's almost like a *snarl*.

"Yes, good girl," he rumbles, bending over me as he continues working on my clit. Damn, his dirty talk is good, and his praise is sending me shooting up even higher. Every stroke of his cock, every glance of his thumb over my clit, is guiding me toward a light so bright it makes me squint. Pleasure is pulsing through every part of me, making all my muscles tighten, even my pussy.

"There we go." Roscoe fucks me even faster now, setting a punishing pace that has me screaming. I roar toward my orgasm like I'm on a train that won't stop, and soon I'm suspended in air, every bone and tendon in my body tensing to explode. "I want you to soak me again, Emelia. And scream my name while you come."

So I do. Damn it, I do, my climax so blinding and deafening and powerful that it's almost painful, all while I scream his name.

That's when Roscoe lets out a noise I never would have expected: a *howl*.

It's not human, this sound, as I sense his cock growing inside me. Thicker and fuller it becomes, until I wonder if I might just come again. How does one man have this kind of power over me?

The howl echoes around the room as he slams in deep, one more time, and it's almost like something *bigger* than his cock is trying to fit inside me. What does it, what sends me over the edge, is how much wider he is at the base, pushing my edges apart and hurling me into what can only be rapture.

I fall to the bed on my face, my legs wobbly as I try to stay upright for him. Roscoe is panting hard, his fingers clutching my ass so tightly that I can feel his blunt nails. He thrusts once more, and for the first time in my life, I can *feel* his hot cum as it spills out of him inside me.

Good thing I'm on the pill.

That thought registers a little late, but I have my excuses. I'm so spent, though, that I can't even hold myself up any longer. Roscoe slides out of me as I collapse fully on the bed, and he lets out a sharp gasp.

"Damn," he mutters, coming to rest on top of me, my back to his front. He buries his nose in my hair and inhales. "God, you smell good. My room's gonna be covered in it."

I shiver, enjoying the idea that I might leave

my impression on this place, even if I never see it again.

And I have a feeling I won't. Which is, in its own way, depressing. I had something wonderful and life-changing happen here, and there won't be a redo.

Eventually, we roll over onto our sides so he's not crushing me with his body weight. Finally, the booze is catching up to me, and I'm barely clinging to consciousness.

"Thank you," I manage to say, turning over so we can look each other in the eyes. It barely registers that his are bright yellow again. "Best birthday ever."

He snorts, and his thick arms bring me in closer as I snuggle between his pecs.

"I'm so glad," he says quietly. "Happy Birthday, Emelia."

I won't lie. I don't sleep great. I'm drunk as a skunk and thirsty, and I get up after what must only be a few hours, begging Roscoe for water. He stumbles to the kitchen to get me a glass, and then after I gulp it down, we retreat back to the bed where he pulls me into his arms without a second thought.

I'm awake again in just a few hours needing to pee, and then more water before I disappear into the blankets. I forgot how much it sucks having that much alcohol.

Finally, I sleep. I don't know how long, but by the time I wake up, light is coming in the windows rather aggressively. The haze has faded and with it, my memory of what exactly I did last night.

I recognize the window, and then it all comes back. Going to Roscoe's place. Having the most mind-blowing sex of my life.

With my ex-boyfriend's dad.

Shit, fuck, hell. I fucked Jason's *dad*. Mere hours after he broke up with me! Or I broke up with him.

I'm still not sure.

I can't believe myself. Well, actually, glancing down at Roscoe's Adonis-like body, maybe I do. Maybe I understand exactly what I was thinking last night. The way he held my hand when I needed it, and let me cry on his shirt, and made me feel like maybe I was lovable. Like maybe I matter. Like maybe I'm not as worthless as Jason made me think I was.

I wish this didn't have to be a one-time thing, but I know what he's going to say as soon as he wakes up. He's going to say it because we both know it to be true—that this can't happen.

It was one night. Not a mistake, not for me. But maybe it will be for him.

After a time of studying Roscoe's sleeping face, his eyes drift open. He blinks them a few times, then his brows furrow.

"Emelia."

I wonder if he remembers. Is it all a blurry haze? Or does he have sparks of memory like I do, snapshots of an experience beyond anything else in this lifetime?

"How do you feel?" he asks.

"Like my head is killing me," I say, and it's true that the low throbbing at the base of my skull has begun.

"Sorry." He reaches up to touch my hair, then pauses, lowering his hand again. With a sigh, he extricates himself from me and sits up on the bed, ruffling his own mussed hair. He runs a hand down his face, and I hope he doesn't regret it.

"Roscoe..." I begin.

"This can't happen again."

The words are firm and final. When I glance

up at Roscoe, his green eyes are intense, his jaw set.

"Oh." I knew that would be the case, but hearing it said out loud, with so much certainty, kind of hurts. "Yeah. You're right."

He nods, then gets out of bed facing the window. I only get a view of his ass as he starts putting on his boxer briefs and jeans, the same ones he wore yesterday. Looking away quickly, I probably shouldn't be ogling him now that we're... whatever we are. Not what we were last night.

Definitely not that anymore.

My stomach sinks as I get out of the bed, too, and find my clothes where they're scattered across the floor. Roscoe isn't messy at all, but there are a few socks out and an overflowing laundry hamper. Besides that, his room is pretty minimalistic.

Not that I should be taking the time to check it out. I'll never see it again.

The silence hangs ugly and thick between us as I put on my clothes, and now fully dressed, Roscoe leads me through the open doorway, down the hall past the bathroom I used last night, into the living room. I pull out my phone hastily.

"I'll call an Uber. Do you... do you want to share one so you can go back to the bar for your—"

"No."

His eyes are like set emeralds in his face. Feeling ashamed of myself for even asking, I quickly pull up the app, my hands shaking. Shit. I look so pathetic right now.

Then I've called it, but since we're a ways out, it will be six or seven minutes until it gets here. But with the frosty air that's now gathered in this house, I say something like, "Guess I'll be going now," and head to the front door. I don't actually remember, because by that point, I was shutting down.

Now I sit on the front curb, waiting, wishing I had never come here last night.

CHAPTER
SIX

ROSCOE

watch Emelia from the window as she sits on the curb, staring out at nothing. I left no room for contradiction when I told her it was time to go, but she didn't need to wait outside. She could have waited in here. That would be safer.

Instead, I stand there and watch to make sure nothing happens to her until a green SUV appears outside. She checks with the driver, then climbs into the back before the car pulls away.

I'm never going to see her again.

It's a goddamned knife through my gut, just

thinking this thought. The wolf goes apeshit, banging at the walls of his cage deep down inside. We can't have just let her go like that, he argues, but it falls on deaf ears.

This was the right thing to do. Give her no reason to doubt, no reason to even think about calling me again. She needs to delete me from her phone forever and move on with her life.

There is no happy ending with me.

When she's gone, I make myself some eggs and sausage, because I need the fat and the protein after drinking so much last night. It really gets harder with age, recovering from a night like that. I'll feel like shit until Monday at least.

But I make myself go to the gym anyway, and take a long, hot shower in the locker rooms. In my mind, though, I can't stop replaying it—the sight of her on her knees in front of me, my cock sliding in and out of her sopping wet pussy as it squeezed and clenched around me. It was so fucking good, being inside her, making her mine, that I'd been desperate to push myself all the way in, knot and all.

Bad idea, Roscoe.

But already, the swell at the base of my cock is inflating, thinking about what it was like to fuck Emelia last night. I might have been drunk, but I remember every single second of it. How she cried out my name. I don't know where calling her my *good girl* came from, but she had loved that, her pussy pulsing and gripping me tight.

Absolutely fucking magical. And I will never, ever have it again.

All I can do is sigh and turn off the water, unwilling to justify my dick's urges in a public locker room.

I have a full-blown headache by the time I get home, and I guzzle down plenty of water to go with my over-the-counter painkillers. Then I lay on the couch, feeling rather miserable for myself, and turn on the TV.

But I don't absorb any of it. All I can think about is Emelia's hurt face as she left my house, the way her shoulders hunched as she sat lonely on the curb, waiting for her ride.

I wish I could be what she needs, but I'm not.

EMELIA

Arin is the only one who knows what really happened because, obviously, I didn't come home last night. But when they see my haggard face, they just hug me.

"Not a good idea," I say, sniffling.

"Do you want to tell me about it?"

I shake my head. What happened last night... it's precious to me, as much as it is tarred. It's something I want to hoard all to myself, because then I can love it and enjoy it without being ashamed of it.

"It's all right," Arin says, helping me over to the couch. "I'm here if you just want to cry."

I knew it was a one-night stand, but I can't help but feel like I've lost something immense, something that could be the pivot point of my life.

Maybe it's just the post-sex hormones.

I'm starving, so Arin and I go out to brunch and try to make the best of the day, running errands and doing our grocery shopping. I don't hear from Jason, which is more of a relief than anything. Part of me hopes I never see him again.

Though I do really need to go over there and pick up my stuff. He has my favorite pair of hoop earrings and at least a few of my sweaters, not to mention my movies, and also my video games, and...

Shit. It might be harder to extricate myself from Jason than I thought.

But that's stuff that I can walk in, dig through his laundry for, and take home with me. We have one shared streaming account, but I pay for that, so I can lock him out with a password change. At least we don't have a dog or furniture.

Maybe I'm glad after all that we never moved in together.

I'll wait until Monday to deal with Jason. Maybe we can arrange for me to come over when he's at work. It's not like I'm going to steal his spoons or anything—he has nothing I want except my stupid earrings.

Jason isn't the one I'm really thinking about. It's what it means. Without that link between us, I'll never see Roscoe again. Frankly, I should probably just delete him from my phone after what was said this morning, but I certainly don't have the mental fortitude to do that.

Not today. I will. I promise, I will. Just... tomorrow.

I don't delete it.

No, every time I remember to do it, I hover over the button. What if I really needed him again someday? I think that if I had no one else in the world to call for help, Roscoe would come.

That is a strange feeling to have about a stranger. I know that, should all else fail, I could rely on someone I slept with for a single night. But then he would vanish from my life again.

So, no, I don't delete it. I keep him in the back of my mind, especially as I organize getting the rest of my things from Jason. He's flippant in his text messages, giving me vague answers about when I can come over. Finally, I get in my car and drive to his apartment, and bang on the door until someone lets me inside.

"Jason's not here," his roommate, Troy, tells me.

"I don't care." I push past him into the apartment, and he doesn't stop me.

I plow down the hallway toward Jason's room as his other roommate pops his head out of his door. Neither of them gets in my way as I go through his room, finding my earrings, my sweaters, even some coasters that he must have taken from my apartment. I grab a book I lent him that he never read, since he doesn't really read, and start fishing my movies out of the cabinet.

"Hey, we like that one," Troy says, but I shoot him a death glare and he steps away.

They've never seen me like this before—a jilted woman, but not by Jason.

Finally, I get the fuck out of that apartment, hopefully never to see it again.

At least I get to start my new job in a few weeks, after I've gotten up to speed on my greater responsibilities. It's scary, of course, but exciting, too. And the raise definitely makes the commitment worthwhile—as does the new window in my office.

Soon it's September, and already some of the leaves are starting to change. I'm always a little sad when summer ends because I love outdoor adventures and hiking, but autumn is beautiful, too, in its own way.

Then my new job starts, and I try even harder to stop thinking about him. *Roscoe*. I hate that I can't get him out of my head. I hate that I go back to that night over and over, knowing I can't do anything to relive it. It's gone forever, and that finality is crushing.

The month creaks along slowly. I thought that over time, the drunken memory would fade, but that doesn't seem to be the case at all. No, those few bright spots I have remain that way, and I spend a lot of dark, lonely nights riding my vibe while I remember them.

I wonder if Roscoe thinks about me at all. Do I occupy his mind the way he occupies mine? I doubt it. Not with how easily and stiffly he told me off. In the light of day, I must have looked very different to him—like a stupid, sad young girl clinging to someone on the worst day of her life.

Then it's October, and the weather is cooling off fast and the days are getting shorter. I've come down with some kind of cold this week, because even though I'm not coughing, I feel like trash. I'm sluggish and my brain feels fuzzy, and I can hardly focus on the email I've been trying to read for the last thirty minutes.

I tell my boss I'm not well, and she shoos me out immediately, the germophobe that she is. My work has become my everything since that night with Roscoe, because it gives me something to focus on, something to steal that real estate in my mind. I'm not sure what I'll do all day without it.

Back at home, I curl up on the couch with a blanket and turn on the television, hoping that curing my cold requires some tea with lemon and honey and a few hours of true rest. But I'm too hot as I lie there, and so I toss off the blanket, which makes me freeze again.

What the fuck is going on? Maybe it's more of a flu than a cold, I think, as my stomach starts churning. Maybe the honey-lemon tea was a bad idea.

Instantly I'm off the couch, sprinting for the bathroom to crouch over the toilet just before bile explodes out of me. I retch into the porcelain bowl, gasping because there's very little in my belly and all that's coming out is water.

Eventually, the need to puke subsides. I fall to the cool tile floor, pressing my face against it as if to remind myself that I'm alive.

As soon as I can get back to my phone, I shoot a text to Arin to tell them that I am, unfortunately, very sick. Maybe they shouldn't even come home and risk infection.

Sit your ass down and wait
for me.

Their text makes me smile. Arin has a deeply nurturing personality, and I should have known I couldn't scare them off.

When their shift ends at the pizza shop, they come home on their bike as fast as possible, carrying a plastic bag full of different medicines. It's so sweet, even though most of them will do nothing for me.

I do take the cold/flu syrup and the Pepto-Bismol, hoping it will settle my upset stomach and prevent what happened from happening again.

I'm not so lucky, though. I find myself on the floor of the bathroom again a few hours later, Arin stroking my back.

"Never seen you like this before," they say, concerned. "Are we sure it's the flu?"

"I don't know what else it could be."

Arin hums thoughtfully as they help me back to my own bed.

"When was the last time you had your period?" they ask as I dress into my pajamas. "Usually we have ours around the same time, but I didn't notice last time."

I guess that is one thing about living together—we're very apprised of each other's business. I always know when Arin's on their period because there are fresh tampons in the trash. Tacky, I know, but that's just life.

Fuck. Now that I think about it... I've been so preoccupied with my new job and with trying to divorce myself from my memories of Roscoe that I didn't notice. I have gone almost two entire months without a period.

"Fuckety fuck fuck *fuck.*" I sink down onto my bed. "There's no possible way. No. I'm on the pill."

But I remember the way Roscoe unleashed everything when we fucked. The worst part is that Jason and I rarely had sex leading up to the night of our breakup. It had probably been a few weeks at best. There's only one way this happened.

All I can do is break out into sobs. This can't be my life. This can't be real. Not with the man who showed me out of his house that morning in so few words.

Arin rubs my back. "I'll run to the store and get a test," they say quickly, drying my tears before they leave on their bike again.

But I already know the answer. I am so fucked.

CHAPTER
SEVEN

ROSCOE

t's unsettling how things simply return to normal after such a life-altering event. No one at work knows what happened with Emelia that night. None of my friends have any idea. I've kept it completely to myself, hoarding my secret and my memories like a dragon.

But it's also painfully lonely, knowing that I can never tell anyone. Knowing that I'll never get to see or taste or feel Emelia again, and what happened with her can't escape my lips. I'll have to take it to my grave.

I've dated a little since Julie and I divorced, but it's never gone anywhere. I've certainly never had sex like that before, not with anyone. The way I wanted to bury my knot in Emelia and stuff her full of my cum was overwhelming in a way it hasn't been before.

Julie never let me knot her, not after I was changed. But I never craved it with her like I did with Emelia.

Nevertheless, life proceeds. I go to work, picking up as many overtime hours as I can to keep my mind busy. I'm building a decent nest egg, and I've paid off the house and my car. Retirement is ten or fifteen years away, and I want to be ready when the time comes.

Then, on one chilly autumn Tuesday, I get a phone call from an unrecognized number. It's in my area code, so I assume it isn't spam. Maybe a client reaching out. Usually they go through the boss, but sometimes I get direct calls from contractors I've worked with.

"Hello, this is Roscoe Daniels," I say as I answer the phone. But instead of a greeting, there's a long silence on the other end. I can hear someone breathing. "Hello?"

"Hey, Roscoe."

It's a quiet, feminine voice, one that's intimately familiar in my memory.

Emelia. I had deleted her number from my

phone so I wouldn't ever be tempted to call or text her. But here she is, calling me instead, when I thought we had made it clear we'd never contact each other again.

"Emelia." It comes out stiff and harsh, because it's opening up a gaping wound I thought I had stitched closed. "What do you want?"

I hear her choke on the other end.

"I'm sorry," she whimpers. "I'm so sorry for calling you."

Something is wrong. I try to soften my voice as I ask, "What is this about?"

There's a long silence on the other end, her breath speeding up.

"Emelia?"

"I'm sorry," she repeats, the words sticking in her throat as she tries to get them out. "I d-d-don't know what to do."

Dread fills my bones. Maybe she's in trouble. Maybe she's in danger. The wolf rises to the surface in a way it never has before, roaring to go to her, to help her, to get revenge on whoever has hurt her.

"Emelia. Please." I try to sound more comforting. "Tell me what's going on."

She takes a deep breath on the other side, clearly trying to calm herself, too.

"Roscoe," she says in a devastated voice, "I'm pregnant."

My whole fucking world goes white. My vision blurs, and my heart practically stops beating in my chest.

No. No way. This can't be happening. There must be a mistake.

"Jason's?" I don't know why I'm hoping that it's his and not mine. It would be worse for Emelia if that was the case. But I also don't want to even fathom what the other answer would sound like.

"No." I can hear her starting to cry on the other side. "It's not. It's yours. I don't know—I don't understand—I was on the pill—but..." A sob breaks free. "I'm sorry. I'm so sorry."

Why does she keep apologizing? I'm the one who came inside her. I'm the one who was too horny and drunk to even consider using a condom. It takes two to tango, and I was one of those two. The older one, in fact, who should have behaved responsibly and didn't.

This is my fault.

"Fuck," I mutter, rubbing my eyes hard. "Goddamn it."

She cries harder. Shit, I'm only making this worse.

I need to see her. I need to hold her and comfort her and tell her it's going to be all right. We'll figure something out.

"Emelia," I say firmly. "I'm coming to get you. Right now."

"What?" She sniffles.

"Text me your address." I use my bossiest tone, because she responded well to that the night we were together.

"O-o-oh, okay."

"See you soon," I tell her in a softer voice. Then I hang up.

The text message arrives with her address—an apartment close to Elroy's. Without a second thought, I get in the car, set up my phone to give me directions, and take off.

All I can think about as I drive is what this means. I can't believe I knocked up a twenty-six-year-old girl. Fuck me. Fuck me into the sun.

I speed more than I should, as eager as I am to get to Emelia's side. She doesn't deserve this. The choice she's going to have to make is a hard one, and I have to be prepared for whichever path she chooses—which could have an astronomical impact on my life and hers. I've already co-parented with Julie while Jason was growing up, and I know I could do it again, but the idea is more daunting than anything I could imagine.

My hands are gripping the wheel so tight my knuckles are white by the time I pull into the parking lot. I don't even need to look up which apartment is Emelia's because she's sitting on the stairs out front, her head in her hands, her whole body hunched forward and curled in on herself.

"Emelia," I say the moment I get out of the car. Her head snaps up, and her face is blotchy pink, her eyes spiderwebbed with red. She doesn't even greet me, just rises to her feet and wraps her arms around herself.

Fuck. I didn't consider this part. Of course she hates me. I saw her face when I spoke to her that morning in my strictest tone, hoping to cut everything off at the bud. Now that's coming back to bite me in the ass, because she looks fearful as I approach the bottom of the stairs.

That's the last thing I want, for her to be afraid of me. Of what I'll say. Of what I'll do.

I take the stairs two at a time until I'm standing in front of her, and she's backing away onto the landing. But before she can get far, I grab her by the shoulders and stop her. Her eyes grow as big as saucers, and she flinches.

What does she think of me that she would flinch away?

"I'm sorry," she says for the millionth time, ducking her head so she's no longer looking at me. "I'm so sorry."

"Stop." I relax my hold on her, but don't let her go. "You don't have to apologize to me."

"But—"

"But nothing." Gently, so as not to startle her, I raise one hand to run my thumb down her cheek. Seeing her up close again, every protective instinct in me roars to life. I need to comfort her. Make her pain go away. Show her everything will be all right.

As if I've summoned them, fresh tears roll down Emelia's cheeks. She squeezes her eyes closed, buckling forward as a sob takes her. Without preamble, I open my leather jacket and wrap my arms around her, pulling her in close just like I did the last time she cried. She's stiff all over, but I hold her anyway, rubbing her back.

"Don't worry," I say into her hair, cradling her head against me. "We will figure this out. Together. I promise."

At last, the tightness in her body fades, and she collapses into my arms. There we go. I take on her weight as her legs go out from underneath her.

"Let's get you inside," I say. "Sit down and talk, okay?"

She nods, clearly unable to get any words out. I keep one arm around her, supporting her as I twist the doorknob and open it. Then I lead her inside, where a small kitchen sits on the left and a living room on the right. There, that couch is the spot.

I guide Emelia over to it and we sit down together. She draws away from me, bringing her legs up onto the couch to hug them with her arms. It's a defensive position, which the wolf doesn't like. She still doesn't trust me.

"When did you find out?" I ask.

"I called you as soon as... well." She reaches over to the side table and produces a plastic baggie. Inside it is a pregnancy test. It very clearly displays two pink lines side by side.

No doubt about it. She has my baby growing inside her, and she's at least eight weeks along now.

My brain pivots to problem-solving mode. I need to fix this, this lack of trust between us, and show her that I'm here for her no matter what. And then we'll proceed to deciding what she wants to do about it.

"I'm not upset with you," I tell her, turning on the couch so I'm facing her. She keeps her head in her hands, not looking at me. The shame is radiating off her. "This isn't your fault, Emelia. Shit happens. I'm the one who should have used a condom."

She doesn't speak.

"I'm here. I'm here no matter what. All right? We can figure this out together."

"There's nothing to figure out," Emelia finally says, squeezing her knees tighter against her. "I know what I'm supposed to do."

I stare at her, not sure what she means. "'Supposed' to do?"

"I'm supposed to get an abortion, right?"

It's like a fucking punch the way she says it, resigned and defeated. As if it's already decided. As if she has no part in it.

"Why would you say that?" I ask. "Who's telling you that?"

At last, she looks up at me, confused.

"Isn't that what you want?"

What *I* want? I haven't even thought about it.

"What I want doesn't matter in the least in

this situation." I lean down so I can really look into her eyes. They're huge and brown and so devastatingly sad, like her whole world has collapsed around her. "I am here to support you no matter what you choose to do."

She stares at me like I just spoke in a foreign language.

"There's no way you want another kid," she says, voice hoarse from crying.

I shrug. "Again, it doesn't matter. I signed up for anything when we had sex without a condom." I try to keep my voice calm and steady and reassuring. "It's up to you, Emelia."

Somehow, my words make it worse, and she starts bawling all over again. The body is seventy percent water, and it's all coming out of her eyes right now.

"But I don't know what to do!" she cries out, flinging her arms into the air. "You were supposed to tell me, Roscoe. This will change your life, too, if... if..." She swallows hard, her hands curling into fists.

"If you keep it?" I supply in a soft tone.

She nods, turning her head away.

"Yeah, it will. It'll change both our lives forever."

"Then I should get rid of it." Suddenly, her

entire demeanor changes. Her eyes harden, and she returns her feet to the floor. "You don't deserve that."

Most unexpectedly, my wolf *roars* inside me. It claws at the edges of my body, furious at the idea that our baby, the one already growing inside her, might go away. That the seed I've planted in her would cease to exist.

"No." The word just comes out of me. I can't stop it.

"No?" she asks, perplexed.

"Please, don't make any decisions because of what you think I want. You don't know what I want."

But *I* know what I want. I know it right then: now that I've seen her after so many weeks apart, I want her. I need her, in every way, and I can't let her go again.

Neither can I let go of the life we've created together, not unless it's what she needs in her own heart.

"What... what do you want?" she asks, and I don't miss the hopeful note. It gives me an idea of what she's really thinking.

"Emelia." I gently raise both hands to her face, cradling it between them. She leans into me, her eyes closing as she absorbs my comfort. Good. "Since you left that day, I've regretted it. I wasn't willing to admit it to myself, but... it's true. I should never have told you to leave."

Her eyes scrunch closed even harder, as if she doesn't believe me.

"Look at me."

Eventually, she does, peering up at me with tears gathering on her lashes.

"I want you. I want you so, so badly. Whatever you decide, I'm not leaving you. I'm not going to watch you walk away again."

Besides, the train has already left the building. Now I'm imagining her with my baby growing inside her, her belly swelling as it takes shape. Now I'm imagining her with that baby in her arms, sucking on her perfect pink nipples. Now I'm imagining it growing up, learning to walk and eventually going off to school for the first time.

But then, my logical brain kicks in.

Emelia still doesn't know the truth about me, and that truth is what destroyed my marriage. Would it destroy what I have with her, too?

"I want to keep it," Emelia says suddenly. She wipes her face with her wrist. "I don't want to say goodbye."

I smile at her, because it's exactly what I wanted to hear.

"All right, then." I slide my arm around her and bring her in closer, kissing the top of her head. "Then we'll keep it."

And I need to come clean with her—soon.

CHAPTER
EIGHT

EMELIA

'm glad Arin made themself scarce when I said Roscoe was coming over. They had saluted at the door, saying, "Be back at ten." Part of me hopes they finally called Harry.

I'm also glad because I just agreed to have a *baby* with my ex-boyfriend's dad. I just agreed to spend the next whatever months carrying it, then giving birth to it, and then... what? Raising it together? As a couple?

I have so many questions, but I'm afraid of breaking the moment between us and asking them.

Of course, I would prefer if we were together

while having this kid. But we've barely gotten to know each other, only had the one night between us. How do I know we can last that long?

There are so many variables, so many unknowns. I feel like I'm standing at the edge of the sea, gazing out into the vast water with no idea of how to build a boat.

"Come back to me, Emelia," Roscoe says, startling me. He's holding my hand in his, our fingers interlocked. His green eyes are concerned. "You went away for a moment there."

I nod cautiously. "It's just a lot. It's so much. I've... I've never had that kind of responsibility before. Over another whole person."

Roscoe squeezes my hand. "It's a scary feeling, I won't lie. And it's not like it goes away. I'm afraid, too. I'm nervous, too."

Somehow, knowing that he's done this once before and still feels uncertain about it makes me less self-conscious. Maybe it's okay that I don't know everything. All of it is taking a risk—having a baby and having it *together*. We might be totally incompatible. We might be making a huge mistake.

But I was telling the truth when I said I wasn't ready yet to say goodbye. This tiny piece of Roscoe that I have... it means the world to me. I can't imagine what's in there, this new being who is half me and half him. Sure, I've thought about having kids someday. I sort of expected I would with Jason, eventually. I liked the idea of having them with someone I love, who loves me. Someone I wanted so fully, so completely, that creating something made of both of us would feel like the culmination of our lives.

I feel some of that with Roscoe. I may not know all the ins and outs of him—I don't even know what color he likes, but I'm guessing black —but I also feel like I've seen inside him, and I like what's there. I like his soul, which is earnest and good. Truly good, down to the core.

And he wants me, too. He wants me the same way I want him. At least, I think. I think that he's got the same craving crawling under his skin, begging to be let out, because there's a fire in his eyes that reminds me of the night at the club, of the look on his face when I got naked on his bed.

"Emelia." He licks his lips as he says my name. "I want you to know I'm in it for the long haul. I'm committing to this. No matter what happens between us, I'll be there for you and for this kid. Forever."

I can't believe how close I am to crying

again. I've never cried as much in my adult life as I have today, like a wobbly balloon blowing in a breeze.

"Thank you." That's all I know how to say in response. "Thank you for... being you."

Then, I throw myself into his arms. I just need comfort, I just need touch, I just need—

Fervently, Roscoe wraps me up, squeezing me tight against him as if he might die without this. His scratchy face rubs against my forehead, and a ripple of pleasure echoes down my spine. I fall completely into his lap, my arms around his neck, my face buried in the hollow of his throat.

"That's right," he says soothingly. "That's a good girl."

Oh, *fuck*. There's that phrase again, and it's like he has a cattle prod aimed directly at my clit. I gasp and my thighs squeeze together.

Roscoe tilts his head down, one of his hands stroking my back along my spine.

"You have a roommate, right?"

"They're gone," I answer quickly. "Until... ten." I check the clock on the wall. That gives us an hour and a half.

Roscoe follows my gaze, and when I look up at him, his mouth is quirked up on one side. There's a mischievous glint in his eye, and he drags in a deep, long breath, as if he's smelling the air.

"Do you want to show me the way to your bedroom?" he asks, his voice an octave lower and much huskier.

I nod rapidly, and he doesn't release my hand as we get off the couch and I lead him around it to the hall. We pass Arin's door, then the bathroom's, stopping at mine. I have the bigger of the two rooms, seeing that I make more money. I've been thinking of upgrading to a bigger place since my raise, but I like living here with my best friend.

That will probably have to change soon.

Roscoe pushes open the door, his eyes narrowed and focused, showing off his crow's feet. His jaw is clenched, too, like he's about to blow a gasket. When we're inside, he slams the door closed, then turns to face me.

"Emelia, I have to tell you something."

I blink up at him, because I thought we were about to have makeup sex. I was really looking forward to it.

"What is it?" I ask, a bit worried.

He shakes his head. "Just look." Roscoe's fingers drop to his belt, which he unbuckles and removes, tossing it to the floor. Drool pools in my mouth thinking about what's underneath. I didn't get to see him that night, and lordy, how I wish I could have. Now I'll get my chance.

But wait. I'm confused. Why is he taking off his pants if this isn't about sex?

Next come button and zipper, and he removes his jeans, leaving his cock straining inside his boxer briefs. They're plain dark blue, and god, he looks good under there. He's already hard, and just thinking about what that felt like inside me—

He hooks his thumbs into the band of his underwear and pulls them off, tossing them aside.

Shit. What *is* that?

His cock is big, yes. It also looks... strange. At the base is a lump, *two* of them, one on either side of the shaft.

Is that what I felt that night? What he didn't put inside me?

"Yup," Roscoe says, sighing. "That's what got you pregnant."

I don't think he intends it, but it sends a shock of pure excitement straight down between my legs. Yeah, that is how he did it. And I want him again.

"It's weird, yeah," I say. "But you were just born that way, right?"

He stares at me for a long beat, then a laugh explodes out of him. He snorts, buckling forward.

"You are too good for this world," he says, stepping closer so he can lean down and kiss me. That kiss, though quick, is absolutely perfect. "No. I wasn't born this way."

I squint. "Huh? Then how did it happen?"

"Emelia." He turns his head away, staring down at the floor as he continues. "I'm a werewolf."

Oh.

So that's why he hid in the darkness. That's why we did it from behind. He didn't want me to see this and then ask questions he couldn't answer.

"I've never met a werewolf before," I begin unsteadily. I'm not sure what the right or wrong thing is to say here. "Wasn't sure if it was a biting thing, or a thing you're born with."

"You have to be bitten." He sighs, his cock deflating the longer we talk. "I was bitten about... eighteen years ago now. When Jason was a kid."

"Was it voluntary?" I ask.

Feverishly, he shakes his head. "I was on a trip with some college friends. We were back-packing in the Rocky Mountains. We must have gotten too close to a werewolf community when we pitched camp, because we woke up in the middle of the night to our tent being ripped to shreds by a werewolf.

"It was completely out of its mind. Probably one that was just freshly turned. It bit all three of us before the others showed up."

"There was more than one?"

He nods. "Yes, but they were more of sound mind. They took us back to their refuge and patched us up, but the damage had already been done. All of us underwent the change there."

"Wow. That's horrible." I didn't realize were-wolf-ism was quite so violent. "I'm sorry."

He shrugs. "I'm used to it now. I take every full moon off work and go out to the mountains. Pitch a tent, hunt some rabbits, call it a night."

"That doesn't sound too bad!" I sit up, smiling brightly. "You can keep doing that."

But Roscoe just shakes his head, and sits down on the bed next to me, making the mattress sink.

"Not if I'm with you." He leans down and sniffs my hair, then rubs his nose over the shell of my ear. "If I'm with you, Emelia, all I'm going to want is *you*. I will tear apart anything in my way when the moon is full. And then, I'll definitely want to fuck you."

It feels a bit like there's a fire starting in my lower belly. That's all he wants? To have sex?

"You don't want to... bite me?" I ask. "Or eat me?"

He laughs. "I have far more control now than that. I would never bite you. But mate you? Up against a tree in the woods?" He breathes against my ear, sending a shiver down my back. "It would be my pleasure. My desire. My instinctual need."

Damn. It sounds good when he says that.

"Okay."

Roscoe freezes where his hand is roaming up my side. "What? Okay?"

"Okay. If you want to have sex... like that. That's fine."

His brow crinkles. "I don't think you understand, Emelia. It's not just sex. It's—" He stops abruptly, gritting his teeth.

"What is it?" I sit closer. "You can tell me."

"It's why Julie and I got divorced. She was absolutely, one hundred percent not interested." Roscoe curls his hand into a fist, like just the memory is painful. "And you probably wouldn't be either, if you actually saw it."

"Saw what?"

"My wolf form. On a full moon."

"I guess I can't say one way or another," I venture. "Since I haven't seen it yet. But... it's still you, right? And I'm not in danger?"

He shakes his head.

"And all you want is to fuck in the woods?"

This time, he nods.

"I truly do not see the problem." Grabbing his hand again, I lean forward and kiss his cheek. "Can we cross that bridge when we get there?"

Roscoe searches me, his dark salt-and-pepper brows furrowed like he still doesn't believe what I'm saying.

"There is one other thing," he says, reaching down to stroke himself. He puts his hand over the bulbs at the base. "I'm going to really, really want to put my knot inside you. But I need to know... if you want that, too."

"Why not?" I cover his hand with mine. "Does it feel good?"

"It should. I think it will. It's... supposed to."

I grin up at him. "Then yes."

"Are you sure? Julie really didn't—"

I silence him with a kiss. Then I lean back and give him a solid glare.

"Stop bringing up your ex-wife," I say. "I'm not her, and it's not making me horny."

A laugh breaks out of him. He snorts once more before sliding an arm around me and dragging me in close. "Can't have that," he murmurs, removing his hand so now my palm is wrapped around his dick. "I need you good and horny for what I'm about to do to you."

"Show me." I stroke him from the odd base up to the tip, admiring the shape of him, how deliciously perfect it is. "Show me what you want to do to me."

CHAPTER
NINE

ROSCOE

Emelia sure took that well. But then again, she has surprised me at every turn. She's so full of heart, so kind and gentle and earnest, that I'm completely enchanted with her. She just wants to feel good and make others feel good, and has no preconceived notions about who I am or who I should be.

She accepts me just the way I am. I suppose we'll see if that lasts through the next full moon. That will be the true test of whether this can work between us.

Just the idea, though, of *having* a life with her, of even attempting one, sends the blood rushing straight down to my groin. Fuck, it's complicated—it's so, so complicated—and yet painfully attractive.

"Take off your clothes first," I tell her, sitting back so I can remove my own shirt. I've been sitting here naked from the waist down for who knows how long, and I want to feast myself.

Emelia nods obediently and gets to her feet so she can pull down her sweatpants, then take off her T-shirt. When she's finally naked in front of me, I grab her hand and pull her closer, wanting to take a big inhale of her. The wolf is pleased with how this has all turned out, and he's quiet as I bring her back down to the bed.

I know exactly what I'm going to do to her.

Once we're lying on our sides, the overhead light still shining brightly down, Emelia licks her lips. She runs her hands down my body, thumbing over my nipples, along the line between my abs toward my belly button. There, she pauses, just studying me.

"You're very pretty," she says, running her hand lower, into my thick, black hair. "Do you know that, Roscoe?"

I shake my head. It's not something anyone has ever said to me.

"You are." She kisses down my chest now

along the same path her hand took, and even though I had a whole plan to fuck her silly and then fit my knot into her, it's out the window as she rapidly makes her way down between my legs. I roll over partway so I'm on my back, and she kneels between my thighs, my cock now thick and full and angling up toward her for her attention.

"I'm angry that no one has loved this well enough," she says, wrapping one hand around the base. Just her fingers on my knot have me twitching underneath her, ready for whatever she doles out. She strokes them experimentally, watching my face as she circles it, squeezes it, strokes it. Everything feels good, though, so I have a hard time telling her what I like best.

And then she does something even better and lowers her head to lick me.

Yep. That's it. My hips jerk involuntarily as she pulls my foreskin down and then licks again, teasing her tongue across my slit.

"You taste good," she says, licking me again. "Really good."

No one's ever said that before, either.

Before I can answer, though, she opens her lips wide and swiftly buries me inside her mouth.

Pure pleasure radiates outward, into my balls, up my spine, all the way to my fingertips. I want to be careful, though, so I just pet her hair, as much as I'm tempted to grab her head and fuck her mouth.

Not that I need to do all that. She does a perfectly good job of setting her own pace, going slow, swirling her tongue around, all while she continues stroking and petting my knot. This woman is going to ruin me, I just know it. It won't be long before she holds my heart fully in her two hands, capable of destroying it with the pinch of her fingers.

Then she speeds up. That's going to be the end of me. Still stroking, she brings me deep into her throat, her tongue constantly teasing and dancing along me. She suctions as she brings me out from between her lips, and I let out a curse because I'm already so close to blowing.

I thought I was better than that. But it's been a rough few months, fucking my hand while thinking of Emelia. Having her here, her mouth sunk down on my dick, pulls on every last thread of my self-control. And if I come now, then who knows when I'll firm up enough to go again, and we don't have much time.

"Emelia!" I hiss, to get her attention, as focused as she is on pleasuring me. "I want you on my face. Now."

She blinks, then grins with my dick still in her mouth. She withdraws it and sits up, lifting herself onto her knees and navigating her way toward me until she's hovering over my face, and I think she's shaking a little.

"Have you ever done this before?" I ask, horrified already at the answer I might get.

"No." She says it meekly.

I grab her by the hips and yank her upward, so her legs are spread around my head and her pink pussy is right over my mouth. She squeaks as I bring her down toward me and lift my head to bury my tongue inside her.

"Oooh." Emelia bucks forward when I suck on her clit. "This is... magical. Your stubble feels..." She rocks on top of me. "That's so good!"

I love that I can do something new with her, when to me, it all felt like it's been done before. But licking her, tasting her, sucking up each of her moans and turning them slowly into cries—that is all beautiful and fresh.

I lick her faster, harder, circling her clit and then jamming my tongue inside her, twisting it to open her, my cock throbbing and leaking just thinking about how I'm going to stretch her out for me.

It will be even trickier to fit when I'm not in my human form, but we'll deal with that later.

Emelia uses me to gratify herself, rocking forward into my face, lifting and then sinking down on my tongue. I let her, squeezing her soft butt with every motion, driving her closer and closer.

Now. It's time. When she goes off, I want her to do it around my cock. I want my knot to be spreading her open, squeezing inside her, bringing her even more pleasure.

I grab her by the hips, stilling her.

"Emelia," I growl, no longer able to keep my voice in check. "Get on my cock. Now."

She hastily obeys, sliding off me, and I find her face flushed bright red. I grab her hips to help her, and soon she's up on her knees straddling my waist, that perfectly pink, swollen pussy almost where I need it.

And do I need it, more than I've ever needed anything.

"Do you have neighbors I need to worry about?" I ask as I stroke myself once, twice, then rub up and down her puffy labia.

Emelia shakes her head. "There's an old guy

next door, but I don't think he can hear. And the people downstairs are never home."

Good.

With that, I grab her ass and guide her down, so the angled tip of my cock slides in. Just the sensation of entering her, of that head slipping through into that warm, wet place, almost does me in. And hell, is she tight, tight and small, which will be tricky to navigate in my other form.

When I was drunk that night, I didn't really get to appreciate Emelia the way she should truly be appreciated. Now I can, memorizing every detail of her, how her breasts look in my hands, her nipples taut and hard; how her pussy has a perfect texture inside it, rippled and such a close fit; how her eyes close the moment I slip through, and her moan flows like water from her lips as I glide in deep on the first thrust.

"Roscoe!" She clutches my chest, snagging some of my hair there in her fingers. "Oh, god, that's good."

I like that she talks to me, telling me what she likes, though I haven't done much of anything yet.

Yet.

Lifting her up, I push my hips down into the

bed, then jerk back up, burying myself in her again. She braces against me, her head tipping down so her hair—that beautiful auburn hair— slips over her shoulder.

"You're beautiful," I tell her, maintaining this slow pace. "You're fucking magical, Emelia. Something I didn't know I needed, and now I'm never going to let you out of my sight."

I must be saying the right words because she squeezes around me and her head falls back. Kicking it up a notch, and controlling her with my hands on her hips, I speed up my pace. I'm still going deep, still keeping my strokes measured and even. When her moans rise in volume, I crank it up even more. I need to make her come at least once before my knot will fit.

"Find it," I demand of her, fucking my cock into her. "Find where it feels best."

She nods rapidly as she tilts her hips. I sink in again, and again she tilts, again she rises and falls, again she sucks me inside her and clenches wonderfully all around me.

"There!" she moans. I lift her and then slam my cock into her at exactly the same angle as before. This time, she cries out.

"Good girl," I tell her, keeping our pace with

one hand while I squeeze her nipple with the other. "Use me until you come."

She takes over guiding us, lifting herself up and then dropping down again, making her own bones rattle with the force of her pleasure. I play servant, going where she needs me to go, taking the pressure off her thighs as I raise and lower her.

"Oh, Roscoe, I'm going to—" She drops again, and I see she's losing control. I take over, lifting her up faster, slamming my cock into her, her breasts bouncing with every thrust. "Yes, yes, that's it, that's—"

She clamps down, and her mouth falls open in a wordless scream. I fuck her still, my cock barely able to move with how tight she is. And somehow, my knot is starting to fit through.

Once her orgasm has rendered her limp and boneless, I flip us over. Now she's at my mercy.

I pull Emelia's thighs apart. But before settling, I put a pillow under her head, and she giggles.

"Thank you."

I grin and kiss her furiously. Just getting to do this, to taste her mouth, to love her lips is a gift I never expected, never could have dreamed of receiving.

"Now I'm really going to fuck you," I tell her, our noses just barely touching. "I'm going to test how much that old guy can hear." I lower my voice, whispering, "And then I'll put my knot into you, and see how you like that."

Emelia's eyes are bright and shining as she says, "Show me. Show me everything."

CHAPTER
TEN

EMELIA

'm still spasming from the force of my orgasm when Roscoe kneels between my legs, his cock thick and heavy, his incredible abs rippling as he positions himself. I just want to eat him with how good he looks, that smattering of hair on his chest, the stubble that's almost advanced to a beard.

Then, he lifts my thigh over his elbow, using his other hand to guide himself inside me. And god, he feels incredible, so fat and swollen with how tight I am from my climax that I moan the moment he pushes through.

"There we go," he murmurs, sitting back on

his knees. He goes surprisingly slow, fully encasing himself in me before drawing back, then shoving himself in as far as he can go. Those bulbs at the base of his cock are already making themselves known, gently applying pressure with every thrust. He slows even further, fisting his cock and swirling it around as if coaxing me open.

Roscoe's voice is raspy as he says, "Relax for me."

I try to do as I'm told, steadying my breathing and relaxing my muscles as he tries again, pushing in deep, that bulge applying so much pressure to my pussy I might just break. But he's never forceful, simply pumping his hips slowly and deliberately, and it's so exquisite that shocks of bliss are pulsing through me.

But I'm still not spread enough to let him through. Releasing my thigh, Roscoe drops forward onto his hands, so now our bodies are pressed together and his delectable face is only inches from mine.

"What a wonderful woman you are," he croons, smoothing one hand down my chest to my belly. "Carrying my baby. Right here."

I didn't think he would bring that into his dirty talk, but it utterly electrifies me.

"Right there," I whisper, wrapping my arms around his neck to bring him even closer while my thighs encircle his hips. Roscoe groans, and his knot applies even more pressure. Slowly, my body parts for it, as slick and soft as I am. Only a little at first, but it's enough to send me sky-rocketing as the bulges press through, stretching me as far as I can go.

"Yes, Emelia." He kisses my forehead, then my cheeks, then my nose and lips. "Let me in-side you. All of me."

I need it so desperately that my body obeys. His fat knot squeezes in, until suddenly it's in-side me, and I'm so completely, utterly full that I cry out his name.

"What a good girl." Roscoe curls his arm under me, holding me in place as he pulls back out, then shoves that massive thing back in. Holy hell, I've never felt anything like that. I'm already so close again. His cockhead stimulates my G-spot while his knot stretches me open, and every muscle and tendon in my body is taut as a wire.

"Look at you," he says in my ear, "taking me so well."

All I can do is whine helplessly as he fucks me faster, that knot slicking in and out in a torturous, beautiful motion. I feel like I might just combust, my whole body begging to release this incredible, glorious, overwhelming pressure. If the world ended right now, I would be happy I had this with Roscoe. Even if I were dead, I would never forget it.

"I'm—I'm—I'm—" I can't even form a sentence with how far gone I am. "I'm going to—Roscoe!"

He clutches me tighter, moving faster now, that fat bulge squeezing through and then pulling back, making a wet popping sound with every pump of his powerful hips. God, his ass, his chest, his abs, his *face*—I can barely stand it, how much I already adore this man, how wonderful and yet terrifying the idea of raising a child with him is.

That's it. That's the thought that makes the world go dark and the pleasure to explode outward like a bomb going off. I scream as it takes me, whirling me into oblivion.

"Oh, fuck," Roscoe says, his voice almost sounding panicked. "God, you're perfect, you're so fucking perfect." He lets out the same animalistic howl as the last time, and it echoes around the room as he continues his rapid pace. Then, suddenly, he jams himself in deep, and my orgasm rears up even greater, even more magnificent.

I think I'm going to die with that knot buried in me. I clamp down tight around it, and I *feel* it as he comes, releasing heat deep inside me. There's so much that I sense a growing weight there, and Roscoe's cock is wedged inside me so tight that nothing can escape. I moan, my pussy desperately trying to eject him as it clamps down, but he's not going anywhere.

"Yes, Emelia, milk my knot." Roscoe is panting hard, chest heaving, my breasts squashed by his body weight. I'm so blissed-out, so exhausted from everything, that I can't utter a word. All I can do is look into his green eyes, which are so soft, so warm, that my heart constricts.

We stay like that for some time, merely looking at each other, his knot still wedged inside me. It's larger than it was when he first pushed it in, and I can barely stand the stretch.

"How long does it... stay like that?" I ask, hoarse from screaming.

"I don't know." Roscoe bites his lip. "I've never knotted anyone before."

Right, I'm his first time.

"Eighteen years you've waited?"

He leans down to brush his lips over mine. "Eighteen years. For you."

Curling his arm underneath me, he holds me even closer as he keeps himself propped up—and not crushing me—with the other arm. And still, the knot remains seated, and no matter how hard my muscles push, he stays there. It's strangely comforting to still be connected, like we don't have to end this just yet.

"Emelia, I think you should move in."

I didn't realize I'd started drifting off when Roscoe speaks. I blink open bleary eyes. I've cried too much today.

"To your house?" I ask.

"It doesn't have to be now. But... if you want to. Of course. Only if you want to. I would just... I would like it if..."

I've never heard him so uncertain. Usually Roscoe is confident, if a bit rough.

"Sure." Maybe I haven't thought of all the angles of it yet, but I love the idea. Moving into Roscoe's little home, setting up a room for the baby, sleeping in the same bed? "I have to sort some things out, find a new roommate for Arin. But I would love to live with you."

He sighs with pleasure and plants his lips on my forehead. "Thank you. It would give me a lot of peace of mind if you were there with me. If I could watch over you."

I think I understand. His instinct is to protect us now.

"I want to experience it with you." I run my hand over the stubble on his cheek, luxuriating in the scratchiness. "Having a baby."

"I want that, too."

After a few more minutes, I sense his knot releasing, and slowly, he slides out. I gasp at the rush of cum that spills down, and I quickly sit up to look. It's all over the comforter, so much I'm shocked by it.

"If you weren't already pregnant, you probably would be soon," Roscoe says with a snort. "That's what the knot is for."

"For... knocking me up?"

He nods. "That's how the internet explains it. Keeps all my cum inside you." He tucks me in against his side. "And I'm going to knot you constantly, Emelia."

I shiver. "I don't mind that." It felt absolutely spectacular.

Eventually, though, I notice that it's nearing ten o'clock.

"Roscoe?"

His eyes slowly open, and he gazes over at me with a smile on his lips. "Yeah?"

"Will you stay over? Tonight?"

That smile widens. "Of course." He turns so my head is on his arm, and his other hand is slung over my waist. I revel in all the places we touch, everywhere his warm body meets mine. "I would love to."

So I get up and switch off the light, then write a quick Post-it note to Arin and stick it on my door, telling them that we'll talk in the morning.

When I climb back in bed, I think Roscoe is already asleep, until his arm darts out and pulls me back down to him. Then he covers us with the blankets, and it's easy to drift off, tangled up in his embrace.

ROSCOE

This woman. Lovely and accepting, open and warm, genuine and adventurous. She breathes a new life into me that I didn't know I was missing.

I get up early to get to work on time, still wearing my clothes from yesterday. Emelia rises with me, offering me a bagel with cream cheese before we both head off to work. We agreed to meet tonight at my house to have a deeper discussion and start making plans.

Light as air, I head off to today's work site. I'm there in my physical body, having conversations, doing my job, but mentally I'm completely in the clouds. Goddamn, I'm almost fifty years old and I'm having a baby with a woman half my age. I must be insane. Completely lost my marbles.

What will Jason say? I don't even want to think about Julie when she inevitably finds out. And my friends, mostly gruff older men like me, who meet at the bar for pool? They're going to drag me over the coals. Sleeping with a younger woman—my son's girlfriend!—and then knocking her up.

It should look like a disaster, but I couldn't be more fucking thrilled.

It'll be tough, I know. I'm gonna be an old guy before our kid is off to college. I'm gonna be chasing a toddler around on my fiftieth birthday. But god, it sounds like the best thing to ever happen to me, getting to do that with Emelia.

I get a text message partway through the day from the very subject of my thoughts.

Sick as a dog.

Poor thing. She mentioned that her morning sickness is what set off finding out about the baby, and I imagine it hasn't gotten better overnight.

Are you staying at work?

Yeah. Quarterly reports and stuff.

It feels so normal, texting with her while I should probably be working, and I wish I could comfort her through the phone.

I'll cook something good tonight.
What can you eat?

What can I eat? Everything,
usually. Except pineapple. Makes
my mouth break out in hives.

Noted.

I smile down at the little glowing screen. My new girlfriend is allergic to pineapple.

Is that what she is? Already it feels like something much greater than that.

"Roscoe," prompts one of my coworkers. "Plan on joining us anytime soon?"

I stuff my phone in my pocket, and he raises an eyebrow at me. "Coming."

"You have a dopey look on your face."

"Met someone," I say by way of explanation, and that's all he needs to chuckle and wave for me to follow.

All day I think about what I could cook, then hit the grocery store on the way home to stock up. We'll go with triple-dipped fried chicken and see how she feels about that. I know it's her favorite.

Around six-thirty, my heightened hearing picks up a car approaching. A sporty sedan pulls into my driveway, and when it turns off, the subject of all my thoughts steps out.

Mine, says the wolf immediately. He's been rather uppity lately, despite it being a new moon tonight.

I head to the door and open it for her, and a radiant smile covers Emelia's face when she sees me. To my surprise, she throws herself into my arms, burying her face in my chest.

"It's good to see you," she mumbles into my shirt, and I laugh.

"Good to see you, too. I'm sorry you weren't feeling well today."

"All better now."

I lead her inside, and both the wolf and I are pleased that she's here with us again.

Right where she belongs.

CHAPTER
ELEVEN

EMELIA

Having dinner at Roscoe's is... wonderfully normal. Salem the cat winds around our feet while we eat, begging for attention. After we devour the amazing meal, we sit down at the table together and work through all the details.

I have some time left on my lease, another month and a half. That's a good point for me to move out of my place and into Roscoe's house. I've already talked to Arin, and they understand why I need to do this—why it's the right move for me and the baby.

"Going all in, huh?" they'd said, one brow

lifted.

I shrugged. "All or nothing, I guess."

Roscoe plans to remove everything of Jason's and give it back to him in a box so we can use his room for the nursery. That's going to be weird beyond reason, I know. I am not excited about the moment we have to come clean, and I'm not looking forward to the rest of my life having to be his... what, stepmom?

Horrifying, actually, when I think of it like that. So, instead, I won't. Jason is just an unfortunate appendage to making a life with Roscoe.

Then there's the matter of telling, well, everyone else. My parents. My older sister, Natalie. God, she's going to judge me so hard, I can feel it from across the country. My friends will probably be the easiest to sell on it.

Not like anyone has a choice in the matter. This is my life, my decision.

"My parents are both out of the picture, if that helps," Roscoe says after I've unloaded my long list of players. "Nobody to disapprove from my end, except maybe my brother." He shrugs. "Rory usually stays out of my business, though. He's too busy with his own life."

Wish I could say the same for my family. My parents are pretty easygoing people, still married and happy after whatever number of years, but they're not going to take it well. Sure, they didn't much care for Jason, but they won't be happy to learn that I'm having a surprise baby with a man almost twice my age who happens to be Jason's *father*.

Oh well.

"They're going to ask the question," I warn him as we finish cleaning the dishes together.

"What question?"

"The 'M' question."

He cocks his head as he dries the pan. "Oh, getting married?"

I nod but don't speak, because I didn't want to broach it myself. I don't even know if I'm ready for that yet, but I'm certain my parents will pressure me to do it. If they can get past the "I'm having a surprise baby" part.

"Well, I guess it depends." He sets down the pan. "I would say, *let's not rush into anything*, but we are kind of gunning it already."

"Yeah. That train left the station."

"We should wait a couple of months. Make sure that you living here is going to work out. Get used to each other."

That's all pretty reasonable. Hopefully my folks will see it that way.

"Great." I turn off the faucet. "Does this mean we've done the hard stuff and we can go to bed now?"

I think my question genuinely takes Roscoe by surprise, because his answering grin is big and unguarded.

"Definitely."

That night, we have sex for hours, and he knots me not once, but twice, until I think I might not be able to walk tomorrow. Then Roscoe lends me a book and we both read for a while before turning out the light.

I could get used to this.

My friends are first on the list, because they're the easiest. Practice, I'm telling myself.

First, I tell the Kims while we're at work. Kimmy's snakes all rear back and hiss at the same time.

"*What?*" she demands, dragging us all into the copier room and shutting the door. "You fucked Jason's *dad?* And then got *pregnant?*"

Despite the door, I'm sure half the office can hear her.

"Shh," I whisper. "And also, yes. I'm moving in with him in December."

"No fucking way," mutters Kim. "Is this a prank? Are you playing a prank on us?"

I shake my head. "Can't fake the puking, unfortunately."

In the end, they both give me congratulations.

"I mean, he seems like a great guy," Kimmy is forced to admit. "Definitely better than Jason."

"He's really something special. Truly. And, uh..." I rub the back of my head. "He's also a werewolf."

They both stare at me.

"Well, then," Kimmy says haughtily. "Can't be all bad."

Becks and Harry have very different reactions. We meet up at Elroy's, and they're both perplexed when I just order a water. The moment I tell them the Cliff's Notes version, they both lean in.

"How did it happen?" Becks asks. "I saw you dancing and wondered if that might... you know."

"You two were pretty chummy," Harry agrees.

I explain in what is probably far too much

detail exactly how things went down. Their mouths fall open when I tell them about how I left that morning, certain I'd never see him again.

"Damn, Dad doesn't play around," Harry says. "Harsh."

I'm agreeing with him when I notice a familiar head of dark hair. And a familiar pair of shoulders.

Shit, it's Jason sitting at the bartop.

I lean forward to whisper to my friends that he's here, when I accidentally knock over my water with my elbow. It splashes everywhere, causing Becks to yelp with surprise and leap out of her chair as it hits her. Every head in the bar turns toward us, which of course, includes Jason.

Great.

Martin runs toward us with towels to help mop up, and Becks heads to the bathroom to try to save her shirt with the hand dryer. I'm the one who spilled it, and I didn't get a drop on me.

"Em," I hear Jason's smooth voice say over my shoulder as I try to clean off the table. "Haven't seen you in a while."

Why is he even talking to me?

"No kidding." I turn around and put some

space between us. "Probably because you never called or texted me."

"I'm sorry about all that." He looks, for the first time, like he might be ashamed. "I don't know what was in my head. I've been waiting for you to show up to Elroy's so I could try to apologize to you in person."

This is the absolute last thing I need right now.

"Apology not necessary," I say, handing the wet towels back to Martin.

"Yeah, it is necessary. I was a major fucking asshole." When I still am not paying attention to him, Jason grabs my arm.

Instinctively, I rip it away, glaring at him.

"You were an asshole. Still are, I guess."

"I'm sorry, Em," he says, though he looks more angry than sad. "I really am. I can't believe I threw away four of the best years of my life. I... I want to try again with you."

I feel like I'm in some kind of weird nightmare. Is Jason really trying to apologize? To *get back together* with me?

I can't help but laugh. I laugh and laugh, and Jason is staring at me like I have an extra pair of eyes.

"You can't be for real," I say. "Months of silence, and now you're saying it was the best four years of your life? Well, it was probably the worst four years of *my* life."

I don't know where this is coming from, but right now, I don't give a shit about Jason. I couldn't care less what he thinks, what he wants, what he was doing that night on speakerphone. He gave me something I could never have dreamed of by standing me up.

"That's not true," Jason says, affronted. "You were in love with me."

"Not really." That's why I didn't care as much as I should have when he was off doing his own thing. "I don't think I was ever in love with you. Not with how you treated me."

The bar is quiet as everyone watches this unfold. Martin returns with a new glass of water, and Jason's eyes track it.

"Not drinking?" he asks in a dangerous tone. "Unusual for you."

Fuck. I did not want to do this now, especially not without Roscoe here. I really should delay it, wait for a moment when we can tell him together.

"None of your business. Are we done yet?"

"Really?" Now Jason is getting madder.

"You're just going to turn your back on me, after all the time we spent together?"

"Yes, I am. I have something else now." I know I shouldn't goad him, but god, it feels good to watch his face like he doesn't understand the words I'm saying. I'm insulted by how baffled he looks, as if I could never find someone else besides him.

"What? With who?"

Harry and Becks both suck in a breath. Jason looks at them, then back at me, his brows lowering.

"With who, Em?" he repeats.

Not that it's any of his business, but I want this to be over. He needs to know exactly where he stands with me.

I clench my fists as I say, "With your dad."

Nobody in the bar says a single word. Jason searches my face like he's waiting for the joke, but then he doesn't see it. No, his eyes widen and his mouth falls open.

"And you're drinking water because..."

I shrug. "Do I have to spell it out?"

He jerks back as if he's been hit with a whip. I could almost laugh at the look on his face, horrified and bewildered all at once.

"That party where you never showed up," I

say, taking a step toward him. He takes a matching one back. "Guess who was there for me? Who supported me when you were fucking around with other people?"

"No way." He shakes his head furiously. "You're *my* girlfriend. What the fuck?"

"I'm not your girlfriend." I scoot my chair back in, waving a hand at him. "Are you done yet?"

"Of course I'm not done!" Jason bellows. Martin runs out from behind the bar, poised to act as Jason's voice rises. "You're fucking my *dad*! And what, having his kid, too? This can't be my life." He stumbles back, rubbing his hand over his face. "I can't fucking believe you. You disgust me, both of you."

"You need to leave," Martin says, approaching him calmly. "Right now."

Jason looks ready to punch him. "Fine," he snaps. "I'll go. I don't care about this stupid fucking bar anyway."

Then he storms out.

Shit. That is not at all how I intended this to go. I hope Roscoe doesn't change his mind about me when I tell him what I said here.

Becks and Harry slap me on the back as they take their seats, too.

"Didn't think you had that in you," Harry says proudly.

"Me, neither." I'm aghast and ashamed of myself, but strangely... it feels good. Like I did something I've needed to do for a long time.

That night, I tell Roscoe exactly what happened, word for word. He sighs as I talk, and I'm sure that he's deeply disapproving of how I handled the situation.

"I'm sorry," I say at the end. "I know I should have been the adult, but—"

"You had every right to do what you did. I'm glad you put him in his place." He shaved recently, which is an interesting development. It shows off his chiseled jaw even more. "It'll make our next family get-together a little... interesting, but it had to come out one way or another."

He pulls my chair closer and slings his arm across my shoulders, kissing my cheek.

"You're not mad?" I ask.

"At you? No. At him? Absolutely. Grabbing you in a bar is inexcusable. I'm glad you taught him a lesson that I clearly didn't."

"Hey, don't blame yourself. Jason is his own person." I take Roscoe's hand and guide it down to my belly. "Just like this will be a person someday with their own thoughts and feelings. But you have to love them anyway, and you love Jason, don't you?"

Roscoe exhales. "Yeah. I do. I love that damned kid."

"I know."

CHAPTER
TWELVE

ROSCOE

Of course I'm proud of Emelia for standing up for herself. If anyone needed to get that out of their system, it was her. She's been walked over for years, and it was bound to explode at some time or another.

I'll deal with all the shrapnel later. Jason needs to cool down for a while, and then we'll talk about it like adults. He does have one good quality, and it's that he doesn't take things in life too seriously, so I think we can iron this out.

My friends took the news about Emelia and the baby with mixed reviews.

"You sure you want to do all that again?" says Greg, a bigfoot I know from an old job working construction. "The toddler years? That shit is exhausting."

I know it'll be a challenge, but I'm excited for it. And doing it with a woman I love as much as Emelia? It's like the life I never got to have the first time around.

"I dunno," says one of my other buddies, "I think you're just jealous, Greg."

In the meantime, it's the end of October and we're approaching Halloween. And this year, that also happens to be the night of the full moon.

Great.

I usually try to keep as low a profile as possible when I wolf out. Get away from people, out in the woods as far as I can walk before the change takes over.

But now, things are different. I have this woman to protect, to watch over. The wolf is not keen to leave her on a full moon, when we'll want her the most.

We. I don't always think of us that way. Usually we want different things, but we are united in our adoration of Emelia. And so I propose that we go camping together that night, at a remote site I know about where there shouldn't be anyone else out celebrating Halloween.

"Do I get to wear a costume?" she asks. "I always love wearing a costume."

I don't quite understand the question, given no one else will be around, but I don't argue with the pregnant woman.

"Sure, you can."

She comes up with something cute, an orange dress with a pumpkin face on it and a matching hat. I'm going to rip that dress off her the moment I transform, but she can look adorable while wearing it now.

"It's going to be cold up there," I warn her. "It's the end of October."

"I know, I know." She zips up the puffer coat she has on over her costume. "I'll be fine." I also had her put on running shoes.

"Why?"

"Well, what do you do when you see a big scary monster?" I ask.

"Um... usually, you run." She grins. "But I don't think I'll run from you."

"What if I wanted you to?"

She pauses, staring at me. "Do you want me to run away from you, Roscoe?"

I might as well tell her, since she's taken everything else rather well so far.

"I would love it." I step closer to her, closing the distance between us, then lean down to nip her throat. Her head tilts back, revealing even more skin. "I would love to wolf out and chase you through the woods. I'll even give you a head start." She moans as I nip harder, farther up. "Then, once I track down your scent, I'm going to rip off those pretty clothes of yours, and—" I raise my head so we're looking at each other. "You used the dildo I gave you?"

Emelia's face instantly turns red. "U-um, yes, I did. The two days we didn't see each other, I made sure to do it." She covers her eyes like she can't stand talking about it. "It fit... just fine. After the second day."

"Good." I tried to find something roughly the size of my werewolf form. "Thank you."

"Well, time to go?" she says brightly, I assume so we won't talk about the dildo anymore, and that makes me curious to use it on her sometime in bed. I don't want to have any shame between us in the bedroom.

We head out of the city in my SUV, packed with everything we need for a nice night of camping. Once we leave the valley, we head up into the mountains, and the dark roads are quiet. Most people are in the city partying, not heading out to the middle of nowhere. A deer jumps out in front of us, which scares the bejeezus out of me, but it's gone before we can hit it.

Afternoon wanes, and finally, we reach the campsite. Emelia clearly has experience putting up a tent, which I like in a woman. We get it erected in a matter of minutes, and then unroll our sleeping bags, as if we'll be using them.

Little does she know I'm going to be a were-wolf until the moon sets, which isn't until two or three in the morning. And we'll make sure she's stuffed full of me the entire time.

We spread out to find tinder, then Emelia quickly assembles a pyramid and lights the fire. We cook a dinner of hot dogs and hamburgers, getting ketchup and mustard all over ourselves. I lick it off Emelia's fingers, which makes her giggle with delight, and then we kiss a sloppy kiss.

I feel so young again, being with her. Suddenly I'm twenty-six, too, and learning for the first time what it means to love someone. She's so bright and full of life, simply radiating it, that building a family with her seems like the best idea I've ever had.

As the sun sets, the sky turns darker and the moon appears. Emelia glances from me to the moon and back again.

"The sky has to be fully dark," I explain. "Then it happens. Don't worry when it does."

She frowns. "Why would I worry?"

"I make a lot of noise. It's... a little painful."

Her face twists in horror. "It's painful?!"

"Yeah, I mean, my bones are changing, so are my muscles. Everything. It's all rearranging and then reforming." It's an ugly process, too, so I was hoping I could do it without her watching. But I think it's inescapable now.

"I'm sorry," Emelia says, looping her arm around me. "I'm really sorry this happened to you."

It's been many, many years and lots of therapy sessions since that backpacking trip, but I think this is the first time anyone has ever expressed true sympathy for me.

I hold Emelia closer to me, kissing her hair, grateful for her generosity and love.

"Don't worry about me," I say. "Worry about you. When I tell you to run, you run, okay?"

She peers up at me. "And you won't hurt me?"

The wolf growls. He would never.

"No, I won't hurt you. Not unless you want me to."

She doesn't react immediately, like I expected. No, Emelia thinks for a moment, and then says, "Okay. Do you have a first aid kit?"

"In the camping box."

"Then you can scratch me," she says, fluttering her eyelashes. "But obviously, no biting."

"Scratching, got it." I bring her even deeper into my embrace, breathing in the scent of her shampoo. "We need a safe word. So I know if it's too much for you."

"Pineapple."

I laugh at her instant answer. "Pineapple it is."

We wait for the milky periwinkle sky to turn fully dark, stars appearing in a wonderful kaleidoscope that simply isn't possible back in the city. We sit on a log together in silence, waiting and watching, until I feel the change begin.

I surge to my feet as my bones start creaking, breaking, moving. I howl in pain as it takes over my body, the sudden need to eat, to devour, to tear and rip. It's always an onslaught like that at first, becoming the wolf.

The ground shrinks beneath me as I shoot up into the air. Even my fingernails burn as they change into claws. My mouth stretches, dragging my jaw along with it and all my teeth as they, too, change and shift into fangs.

Emelia cries out beneath me. I glance down to see her terrified face, her hands extended toward me.

"Roscoe! Oh my god, are you all right?" There's probably some blood on me, like there usually is after I change.

Mate. That's the only thought in my big, stupid head as Emelia looks at me. *Mate her. Breed her. Fill her.* It doesn't matter that she's already carrying my baby.

"Go, run," I try to say to her, and it comes out a rumbling growl. "Run, Emelia."

She remembers what we talked about, turns around, and takes off into the trees, her white sneakers flashing in the moonlight as she vanishes.

As much as I want to leap into action and chase after her now, I need to wait and give her a chance if this chase is going to be fun. I'm panting, sniffing the air, my cock already emerging from its fur sheath as her scent rides on the wind.

I'm going to devour her.

I wait and wait, growing ever more impatient, ever hungrier for my woman. My mate, for life. I know it now that I'm him, now that the wolf and I are one. She's mine and only mine, forever.

Finally, I can't stand it any longer. I have to find her, make sure she's all right out there in the dark woods, and then bury my cock in her flawless body.

Dropping to all four legs, I let out a powerful howl, one that shakes the very trees. Then I take off into the woods.

EMELIA

Oh my god. I'm running from a fucking werewolf.

Yep, that was a real werewolf all right. Roscoe changed right in front of me, rising high above me, his bones snapping and then reforming, a tail erupting from his spine, ears rotating and then growing up into fluffy points. His mouth warped into a snout, his teeth becoming deadly fangs.

He is fearsome, with a dark coat the same

color as his human hair and some silver around his muzzle and chest. His claws are like black daggers, and I almost regret the thing I said about scratching. His big nostrils had flared, breathing in my scent, and yellow eyes peered down at me as his tail twitched.

Then he told me to go, so I went.

Now I'm dodging tree after tree, hopping over logs and rocks, making my way along the side of the mountain. I'll waste too much energy if I go uphill, so my best bet is to stay on flat ground and try to save my strength. I'm pretty fit, and I think I can get well ahead before he—

Then I hear it, the howl not that far off in the distance. Shit. He's that close already?

I speed up. Now I'm flying over the terrain, eating it up, my heart rate skyrocketing. Then behind me, I hear panting through the trees. A roar fills the woods, and then I remember it: the dildo.

Jesus, it was big. When Roscoe gave it to me, I thought he was joking. When I realized he wasn't... I might have second-guessed all this. But I knew I couldn't do that, so I took the dildo obediently and started working my way up to it.

I had seen his cock as it started emerging,

and it's no joke. It was slick and red and shaped to penetrate.

I'm ready, though. That creature back there was most certainly Roscoe in his rawest form. And he's going to chase me through the woods and fuck me, probably on the forest floor.

Despite the racing of my heart, the pounding of my pulse and the drumming of my feet, I'm warm between the legs thinking of my Roscoe, my calm and sturdy man, roaring like an animal as he bounds behind me. The sound of his feet churning the pine needles surrounds me, so I don't know which direction he's coming from.

"Found you," a deep, rumbling voice says. I stop in my tracks as he emerges from the woods in front of me, as if he ran an entire loop around me. He's on all fours, fangs dripping with drool, his eyes glowing in the night. His tail thrashes as he rises to his feet, towering over me.

That cock is fully protruded now, shining in the moonlight. Everything glows silver as Roscoe lowers his head toward mine.

"Get on your knees." It's almost difficult to understand him through the werewolf's jaws and teeth. "Now."

I won't argue with him on that. I peel down my leggings to my knees, then get down on the forest floor. Pine needles bite through the leggings, but at least I have some padding there. My hands aren't so lucky.

Roscoe snarls, then drops to his four legs again behind me. What I don't expect is the huge, wet tongue that lances out and drags across my exposed sex.

I lurch forward, shocked at the sensation. Roscoe does it again, licking me from clit to ass and then back. He plays with me, that big tongue doing absolute wonders.

And then, he drags it down and shoves it inside me.

"Oh!" I sag forward, not expecting that. Holy shit, though, does it feel good. It twists and rubs inside me, and I'm twitching and moaning as he delves deeper with it, pushing me open even wider.

Then, abruptly, he leaves me. Big, clawed hands land on my ass, and the wolf crouches behind me. His drooling cock is searching, smearing pre-cum all over me, until finally, he finds what he's looking for.

It's just as massive as he prepared me for. The sloped tip easily slips through, as recently as I used the toy he gave me. But the deeper he goes, the wider he is, until I don't know if I can take any more. Just before I'm about to beg him to stop, he withdraws, giving me a moment's rest.

Then he pushes in more. And more. Roscoe is growling on top of me with every thrust, muttering something guttural that sounds like my name. Claws dig into the flesh of my ass, dragging up my back and surely leaving marks. I moan at the pain, at the stretch, and he's pulling me deeper and deeper into the pool of our pleasure.

"Mine," Roscoe snarls, thrusting in a wild, feral rhythm. "All mine."

I nod rapidly. "All yours," I echo, and he howls.

EPILOGUE

ROSCOE

Soon it's December, and Emelia's lease has run out. She's been slowly packing up her things, but that night, Harry, Arin, and I work together to carry all of her boxes of mementos, books, and mysteriously, her favorite college papers, across town to my house. Then we buy everyone pizza.

I enjoy standing in the doorway while Emelia places each of her books on my bookshelf, making sure they're all in the proper order. She sets right away to putting pots of flowers around the house without telling me, so they just appear one day on the front step—bright pops of color that bring a new life to my little home by the railroad tracks. She even buys Salem a new cat bed he probably doesn't need.

Thankfully, Emelia's morning sickness abates after a few more weeks. She gets wild cravings, and it's always an interesting challenge heading to the store after work so I can best figure out how to utilize pickled peppers.

Tentatively, I reach out to Jason to make holiday plans. We always get together for Christmas if he doesn't fly to Illinois to see his mother. I'm also testing the waters to see if he's cooled off enough that we can talk.

I'm surprised when I get an answer right away.

Is she living there?

I wonder if he heard from someone Emelia knows, or if it's just his intuition.

Yep. Do you want to meet up and talk?

Again, the reply is quick and sharp.

The chophouse at nine.

I sigh and put my phone away, telling Emelia the news.

Jason's there already when I arrive right at nine, drinking a beer and eating wings while watching the TV. He doesn't even look at me as I slide into the booth.

"I can't believe you fucked my girlfriend." He barely turns his head when he glances at me. "And knocked her up."

Cold open.

"I'd say I was sorry, but I'm not."

Jason chuckles dryly. "You certainly don't seem sorry. You're grinning like an idiot."

"My coworkers say that, too."

Finally, Jason turns in his seat to face me and cleans his hands on a napkin. At least I taught him some manners.

"And what? You two are gonna raise that kid together?"

"That's the plan."

He sighs and drops his head into his hands. "Damn it, Dad. I'm trying to be pissed at you."

"You're the one who picked up the phone that night in a room full of other women," I remind him.

"Yeah, but my *father* isn't supposed to be the one picking up the dropped ball."

I sigh. "If all you can do is compare a woman to a football, then maybe you should work on yourself some more before you criticize me."

His eyebrows jump. "Damn. You have changed." He tilts his head, studying me. "I guess it kind of makes sense. She was too nice for me."

I nod, because this is true.

"You're supposed to disagree," Jason says with a grunt.

"Sorry. But I've always been honest with you, haven't I?"

With a reluctant sigh, he answers, "Yeah."

"I will say that I'm the happiest I've ever been. Not that you asked."

My son is quiet as he picks up another wing and eats it. Finally, after wiping his hands again, he speaks.

"I can tell. Mom's gonna lose it when she finds out, though."

I shrug. "Oh well. I can wolf out with Emelia like I never could with her."

Jason's brows rise. "She doesn't mind that you're a werewolf?"

"Not at all." I don't go into detail about how much she likes it when I ruthlessly fuck her in the woods.

"I can't believe you're gonna have a baby," Jason says, shaking his head. "I'm going to get a... half-sibling? At twenty-seven? Fucked up, man."

"Yeah, kinda." I take a swig of my own beer, which tastes great because I haven't been drinking around Emelia while she's pregnant. "But sometimes that's how it shakes out."

"Crazy world. Well, I'll come for Christmas, I guess."

I reach across the table to slap him on the shoulder. "Good. Thank you."

He pushes my hand away. "Whatever."

EMELIA

No, my parents are not happy when they find out about Roscoe and the baby. And I still haven't told them he's a werewolf.

But that feels like our private business.

Natalie was, to my surprise, more understanding. We spent a long night talking about what Jason had done, how it all ended up like this, and why Roscoe is the best thing to ever happen to me.

"It seems like you found love in a truly unexpected place," my older sister says. "Well, I'm happy for you, Em. I'll come out for the wedding. When is it?"

"The baby is due in April, and we'd like to get married before that—so February."

"I can't believe it," Natalie says, sighing. "My little sister, having a baby. Excited to see you. I'll be there for the bachelorette party."

The first thing my parents do is hop on a plane to come visit. My dad is all huff and bluster when he arrives, but as always, Roscoe is disarming—unfailingly polite while also gruff, charming as much as he is understated. Before any of us knows it, Roscoe's showing my dad out to the garage and his 1970s project car, and they both start bonding over the slick paint job and repaired leather seats.

Mom inspects every corner of the house in the meantime, then pulls me aside.

"Are you sure you want to do this?" she asks, using that concerned mom voice I know so well. "There are other options. He seems like a good guy, but he's twenty years older than you are."

I shake my head vigorously. "Mom, I love him. I love him so much, more than I thought possible."

She cocks her head. "Really? That much?"

"I'm... I'm really excited to have a baby with him." I put my hand over my stomach, even though there's not even a bump there yet. "I want to do life with him."

She sighs, but I think she understands when she pulls me in for a hug. "Fine. Dad and I will split the cost of the wedding with you. Okay?"

"Thanks, Mom."

It's not Roscoe's first wedding, so he wanted something small and private. I'm not against that, of course—but once upon a time I did dream of having a princess wedding with flowers and a fancy church, so he agrees to a middle ground without much fuss.

Then we start decorating the house for the baby's arrival. We cover the old paint in what used to be Jason's bedroom with fresh paint in a soft, sunny color, getting it all over ourselves and each other. Now, everything seems to be forgiven between Roscoe and Jason, and Jason comes over on the weekend to help us assemble the crib and hang up mobiles.

Yeah, it's weird. It's super weird. But we both try not to make it weird, assuming a stalemate because we each love Roscoe in our own way.

All sorts of other stupid pregnancy stuff

starts to happen, though. I get gestational diabetes, which sucks, the test being the worst part. As I get bigger, my feet hurt more, and I've got to pee all the time.

"Damn baby squashing my bladder," I grump as we watch TV and I get up for the millionth time.

Roscoe chuckles when I come back. "Yeah, everything's moving aside to let baby in. Pretty crazy what you can do."

"True. We made a whole person together."

I'm also horny as fuck, pretty much all the time. I asked him not to shave because something about rubbing his stubble is soothing, and I love when he goes down on me.

And then, that knot. I drool over it. Even in werewolf form, we've worked up to a point where he can start using it on me, and it drives me absolutely mad. It seems impossible, but when he squeezes it inside me, it's all I can do not to come on the spot.

When we have sex, he loves to hold my belly in his hands, caressing my tits as they get bigger. He's obsessed with my changing body, and I think it's made him just as relentlessly horny for me.

"Look at you, getting ready for our baby," he

says, testing my sensitive nipples. "What a good girl."

It always drives me up to the moon when he says that.

We decide to find out the baby's gender, and we're overjoyed to learn it'll be a girl. It also sends Roscoe into a fresh existential crisis over whether he'll be a good dad. It reassures my nerves sometimes to see that he still worries, even though he's the most capable, level-headed person I know.

It's tricky finding a wedding dress that will work with my growing body, but I manage to find something we can adjust at the last minute. The seamstress takes it as a personal challenge.

I feel like a balloon about to pop.

Finally, I get my wish, finding my amazing man standing at the end of the aisle when my dad leads me in. He's impossible not to love, es-pecially with the way he's opened up. He smiles much more often now, which he does when I appear. Chin shaven clean, his salt and pepper hair combed back, his eyes crinkling as I ap-proach... I want nothing more than to jump his bones in that handsome suit.

Finally, all the sermonizing ends, and it's time.

"Will you be my wife?" Roscoe asks, as Jason stands off to one side as his best man. "Forever and ever, until death do us part?"

I blink back tears. "I do."

He rubs a thumb across my cheek, then leans down to kiss me. He gives me all of himself in that kiss, the wolf and the man, until our audience is cheering and flower petals are falling through the air.

The baby comes right on time. My husband is by my side, holding my hand, when little Sofia enters the world. She screams a shrill scream, and we're both relieved to finally hear her voice and know that she's safe and sound.

And she likes to make good use of it. Within a few months, we're run ragged, but at least we can have sex again. When Sofia is asleep, my werewolf brings me into his lap, licking the milk off my nipples. On full moon nights, Arin is happy to watch the baby so we can go out into the woods, where Roscoe chases me until I'm panting and wet, then he snatches me off the forest floor and takes me up against a tree.

"Thank you," Roscoe whispers, nuzzling my nose with his big one as he sinks his knot inside me. "Thank you for being mine."

THANK YOU FOR READING!

If you enjoyed Emelia and Roscoe's story, please consider leaving a review. Reviews are incredibly helpful to indie authors like me in finding new readers.

JOIN MY NEWSLETTER!

For all the latest regarding books, and to get access to a FREE novella, join my newsletter!

www.LyonneRiley.com

Get lots of steamy art to go with your favorite stories! Visit me on Patreon for my latest ongoing serial.

Patreon.com/LyonneRiley

ABOUT THE AUTHOR

Lyonne Riley published her first book at age five, which was written on tiny sheets of notebook paper, and she insisted on giving a copy to everyone she knew. She's been writing ever since, from fan fiction in her teen years to original fiction as an adult. After a stint in traditional publishing, she discovered what she truly wanted to write: very smutty stories about monsters and the little humans they worship.

Now she lives in the middle of nowhere with her dogs and spouse, writing sexy fairy tales.

ACKNOWLEDGMENTS

I would like to thank everyone involved in helping me through the process of putting out this book. I can't say enough how much I appreciate the encouragement of the people around me—especially Amber, who told me I could do this in the first place.

Huge thank you to Rowan Woodcock for the gorgeous cover illustration. A big thank you to Ana Hansen of Sparks Editorial for all her help getting this right, and always Emily Michel for making time for me and my craziness. Thank you to Jenifer Wood for loving this story while I was writing it and encouraging me to keep going. And of course, thank you to my amazing spouse, who has always supported my dreams—and given me lots of inspiration for my characters' sexy adventures.

And thank you to my readers, who gave this little book a shot.